Wyngate Manor

by

June Bradley

Published by
Melange Books, LLC
White Bear Lake, MN 55110
www.melange-books.com

Wyngate Manor
June Bradley

Adrienne Wyngate is jilted on her wedding day. She leaves her Island home and returns three years later where she meets Tyler Prescott, a land developer who she believes is more interested in her ancestral home than her. He believes the tragedies she has suffered through the years are not accidents but murder.

Chapter One

"I can't breathe," Adrienne Wyngate complained.

Hannah smiled at her young mistress as she took several pins from the waist of her wedding gown. Adrienne sighed with relief.

"In three days you will marry the handsome Steven Forrester. It's good you are having your wedding here. This old house needs new blood. We haven't had this much excitement in years. The designers are already decorating the ballroom."

"Thank you, Hannah."

Adrienne wished her family were alive so they could witness her wedding. She and her grandmother were the only surviving Wyngates. Her favorite, Uncle Eric, had disappeared at sea years ago. She believed him to be alive, contrary to the rumors of his death.

"Adrienne, where are you?" Simone, her best friend and Maid of Honor, called from the hallway.

"We're in the sewing room," she answered joyfully.

Simone came into the room. Tall and willowy like sea grass, her dark hair flowed around her shoulders. Her smile had broken many hearts. It included Adrienne's brother, Elliot, when he was alive.

"You look gorgeous." She hugged Adrienne.

"It's all due to Hannah's excellent needlework."

"Every once in a while a miracle like this happens. Your mother would have been happy to know you chose her gown to wear for your wedding. You're going to make Mr. Forrester a very happy man," Hannah said.

"Thank you." She swirled around to get a better view in the long mirror. Adrienne and her friends were so busy talking, they were

1

oblivious to all else.

"Darling, you look ravishing," Steven, the groom to be, said.

Everyone turned and stared at him. Tall with dark hair and eyes, he had the build of a man who was used to hard work. For a moment, no one said anything.

"Did I say something wrong?"

"Go away, go away," Hannah shouted, a look of horror on her face. "It's bad luck for the groom to see his bride in her gown before the wedding."

Simone appeared surprised at Hannah's outburst. Adrienne could tell Steven didn't understand the warning. He was confused, but turned and left.

Adrienne slipped out of her gown, hastily threw on a robe, and ran after him. She caught up with him at the top of the stairs.

"Darling, please wait." She grabbed his arm and turned him around to face her. "Don't be upset. You know the Islanders are a very superstitious people"

"I'm sorry if I upset Hannah."

Adrienne saw his smile reach his eyes. "Our day will be one we'll long remember. Everything will be all right."

"I'm marrying you in three days, and I plan to spend the rest of my life here. I'll get use to their superstitious nature." He leaned over and kissed her. "I've got to run. I only stopped in to see how the arrangements were coming along. I'll see you on Saturday, Cara Mia." He kissed her goodbye.

Adrienne returned to the sewing room and heard Simone and Hannah discussing Steven's unexpected visit.

"It's just an old superstition, Hannah. Modern day people don't believe in those sayings anymore."

"My people do," Hannah muttered.

Adrienne wasn't superstitious. However, she was raised to respect other people's beliefs. Many of the older islanders still adhered to the old sayings. They had been passed down through generations. As she entered the room, Hannah was putting away her sewing kit and was about to depart.

"I'm sorry, Miss Adrienne. I shouldn't have spoken to Mister

Forrester that way." Hannah looked upset.

"It's all right, Hannah. He hasn't been here long enough to understand our people and their customs. It will take time for him to adjust to our ways. Everything will be fine."

Hannah had worked many years for the Wyngate family, so she would have money to buy the medicine her people needed. She shared with her people their beliefs in what their parents taught them. Adrienne hoped Hannah wouldn't worry too much.

The maid left the room crossing herself and muttering. "It's too late. It's too late. Something terrible coming here."

Adrienne responded to the unhappy look in Simone's eyes. "Don't worry. Nothing will happen." She walked her friend downstairs to her car.

"How is Peter taking your engagement and marriage to another man?"

"He seems to be taking it quite well."

"He had hopes of marrying you."

"I know. We're good friends. You've never cared for him."

"Be careful, love." Simone looked uneasy. They both knew several of Hannah's past predictions had come true.

Chapter Two

Adrienne watched her friend drive away. Returning upstairs, she made her way along the hallway to the Great Room. Entering the room, she turned on the lights. Family portraits of all the Wyngates, from the founders of the Wyngate Dynasty to the pictures of recently deceased members, hung in this room. This was her favorite place in the entire house. She could sit here and dream. Most of her deceased relatives appeared to be sleeping.

As a child, she had held conversations with the founders. At present, they were carrying on a lively discussion until they saw her approach. Their discussion ceased abruptly.

"What were you arguing about?" Adrienne inquired. "Why did you stop when I entered the room?"

Theo reacted to Adrienne's questions. "Johnnie thinks you should go to the Colonies for your honeymoon."

Adrienne smiled. "They haven't been called that for a few hundred years. They're the United States of America."

"We were never able to visit," Johnnie told her. "I thought it would be nice if you went there. When you come home, you could tell us about them."

"They're very modern." Adrienne answered, still smiling.

Before Johnnie could reply, Theo interrupted. "I'm so glad you decided on the continent. It has old world charm and is very much like our home here. Of course, I haven't been home in centuries. It would be nice to see it again."

"You wouldn't like the changes," Adrienne replied. "Sir John, you'll be glad to know we haven't had any more prowlers of late searching for your gold."

"My gold and I are safe as long as I'm guarding it."

"What happens if they find gold? You won't have to guard it any longer."

"It depends on many things. You've never been curious about it."

"I have no reason to be. Our Devil's Golden Rum business is thriving. I have plenty of money. The man I'm marrying is also wealthy. I came to say hello and see if you were ready for my wedding."

"Darling, we're looking forward to it. It's been a long time since there's been a wedding here," Theo added.

"I'm wearing my mother's wedding dress," Adrienne said. "Hannah altered it for me. It's so beautiful."

"Oh, darling, I remember it. Your mother will be delighted to hear that when I tell her." Theo smiled at Adrienne.

"It's too bad," Johnnie interjected, "your other relatives can't attend. You, my dear young lady, have love and compassion in your heart. That's more than I can say for some of our offspring."

It was unusual for Johnnie to get sentimental. "Why thank you, Sir John."

"Be on your way, darling. We know you have a lot to do," Theo insisted.

"Are you trying to get rid of me?" Generally, they liked her to stay and talk about the rum business and the plantation, but today they seemed distracted.

"Never. You know us better than that," Sir John replied.

Johnnie and Theo didn't appear as happy as they generally were. Did they know something they weren't telling her?

* * * *

Her ancestors made sure Adrienne was gone and out of hearing range before they continued their discussion.

"Oh Johnnie, do you think we should tell her what we know?"

"We can't interfere with what is to be. You know it as well as I do. It will only make matters worse."

"I don't want her to stop coming to see us." Theo had tears in her eyes. "She's been so good for us."

"I know, my dear. All we know is that something will happen and we cannot stop it."

Chapter Three

"It was a great party. Thank you," Steven told Alex Diego, his old friend, and Peter Llewellyn, a family friend of Adrienne's.

They were the last to leave Steven's Bachelor Party at Jolie's Club. The amount of alcohol they consumed made them a bit tipsy and put them in a jovial mood.

"Welcome to the family," Alex said. He warmly shook Steven's hand.

He was a big man who could be gruff and tender at the same time. He had been married to Adrienne's older sister, Aimee, before her tragic death. He'd become a vital part of the Wyngate family. Alex would have the honor of giving Adrienne away, and her old friend, Peter, was to be Steven's best man.

"Go home and get some sleep," Alex said to Steven. "Tomorrow, you have a busy day ahead of you."

"Take good care of my girl," Peter commanded with a possessiveness Steven hadn't noticed before. Tall with broad shoulders, sun bleached hair, and blue eyes now blurry with fatigue, he owned a ranch in the valley and was one of the wealthy Wyngate clan.

Steven had parked his car in the alley behind the club. Tonight was darker than usual. Somewhat befuddled with drink, he paid little attention to his surroundings. Suddenly, three men attacked him.

"What the devil do you think you're doing?" he shouted.

None of them spoke. He threw a couple of good punches before a blow to his head knocked him down.

Steven took a hell of a beating from the thugs. He remembered leaving the club and that was all. Through his dazed and blurred condition, he heard one of the men speak.

"The boss wants him dead. We'll get good money for this bloody mess."

They dragged Steven to a truck and drove some distance over dirt-rutted roads. Somewhere along the route, he passed out. When he regained consciousness, he tried to place the smells and sounds around him. Nothing was familiar to him.

The truck stopped and the men dragged him from it, throwing him onto rough ground. They stripped him of his clothes, and a sharp sting hit his back. A whip? The sea sounded in the distance.

The whip burned like a hot branding iron. He screamed in pain. No one heard him or came to help. They must be in a desolate part of the island. They broke his left leg with a baseball bat and agony took him. Nothing could relieve his torment, not even the rain that began to fall. The rising wind sent shivers through his body. At last, they stopped and dragged him into the sea.

The cool water revived him. He passed in and out of consciousness. He floated for a while as he felt his body scream for relief. He turned over and floated on his belly.

In the early morning darkness, the wind and the rain slowly subsided, leaving an uneasy stillness. The only sound he heard was the sea calling to him. "Stay with me, stay with me."

"I can't. Adrienne's waiting. I must hurry or I'll be late. I can't let the sea claim me or I'll never see who..."

His memory deserted him. He fought to prevent the sea taking him. He turned on his back again and floated, telling himself to relax and not let go.

"You can stay with me forever and rest in eternal peace," the sea whispered.

"No," he protested.

The sun rose over the horizon. He turned back on his belly and glimpsed, through bleary eyes, an island ahead, or was he hallucinating? He forced his body forward.

"I've come this far. The tide will carry me," he told the sea.

After many hours, by the grace of God, his hands scraped the sandy bottom. The water clung to him like icy fingers as it tried to drag him under and back to sea. He strained and forced himself forward, out of reach of the receding waves. He lunged with the determination of a man who had looked into the oblivion of death. He didn't want to go there again. He dragged his body far enough onto the beach to evade the hungry waves and collapsed on the shore. Every part of him ached in places he never knew could.

The ominous stillness was a warning to ships at sea. The storm wasn't finished with its deviltry. The incoming tide lapped at his body, caressing it like a jealous lover not wanting to share. The clinging hands of death sought its lost treasure, but without success. It wasn't time for Steven Forrester to die.

He lay naked and exposed on the glittering sand. Exhausted from his long struggle to survive, he curled in a fetal position. In a semiconscious state, it felt good to just lie there and relax.

The morning sun rose high in the sky, and he shut his eyes against its hot glare. He heard movement and lifted his head. He opened his one good eye. Two elderly ladies in blue pinafores and white blouses stood nearby, watching him.

"Help me." Then he passed out.

* * * *

After the storm, Sisters Theresa and Josephina began their morning walk, gathering driftwood along the shore.

"Oh, my goodness," declared Sister Josephina.

They stared down at a naked and beaten man lying on the beach. He looked like a plucked goose, unconscious with seaweed, grease, and dirt clinging to parts of his body.

"Sister, stop swooning," Sister Theresa ordered. "You've seen a naked man before."

Dropping her armload of wood, Sister Josephina gasped as she bent down to view the man. She looked up at Sister Theresa.

"Oh dear, what shall we do?"

"Stop gawking at the poor man," Sister Theresa commanded. "Go get the others to help carry him to the infirmary."

She dropped her armload of wood and bent down to feel for a pulse in the man's neck. She was relieved to find a weak one.

June Bradley

"Who are you young man? What did you do to deserve a beating like this?" She spoke in her soft but authoritative voice.

* * * *

Steven struggled to respond to the voice. His eyes fluttered open. He tried to answer, but couldn't. The effort was too much.

A sigh from the person followed. "I'll ask the questions. You nod your head, yes or no. Is that too much for you?" the voice continued.

Pain shot through Steven's aching head. He slowly nodded and winced with the effort.

"Do you know who you are?"

Steven shook his head. Then he put his hands up to stop the pain.

"You've been severely beaten."

He nodded, trying not to lose consciousness.

"Have you any idea how long you've been in the water?"

Steven shook his head. He tried to talk. He wanted to make her understand. He had to be somewhere important, but he couldn't remember why.

Three more people arrived with a stretcher. They gently moved him onto it. In Steven's mind, they blended into a mass of blue.

* * * *

When he regained consciousness, he found himself alone and in a strange place. It looked like a hospital. How had he gotten here?

Chapter Four

Adrienne bubbled with excitement. The wedding invitation she held in her hands announced her forthcoming marriage to Steven Forrester, a wealthy businessman.

From her bedroom window, she saw the wedding guests as they wandered through the plantation's gardens. The peaceful serenity of water cascading from beautifully carved mermaids and other sea creatures to fall into small pools filled with swimming fish made her think of her family and the happy days spent in this house. However, this was no time to reminisce. Far below in the cove, brightly colored yachts lay moored on the calm blue-green sea.

She turned to see her mother's wedding gown hanging on her closet door. She would carry a bouquet of the beautiful Cattleya Orchids that grew profusely on the island. How she loved them.

The caterers and the florist had arrived hours ago. The musicians were tuning their instruments. With her grandmother Charlotte and Hannah's supervision, everything would be perfect.

A knock on the door brought Adrienne back from her musings.

"Everything is so beautiful," her grandmother told her. Charlotte's suntanned face glowed with happiness as she came to Adrienne. "My dear, I have never seen the house looks so enchanting."

Adrienne reached over and kissed her. She knew Charlotte loved her dearly. At the age of seventy-three, Charlotte's life was mostly memories while Adrienne's life was beginning.

"I wonder what's keeping Simone." A sense of unease troubled Adrienne.

"I'm sure she'll be along any minute now. She's as excited about your wedding as you are."

"I wish she'd hurry. I'm nervous." Adrienne pulled at her petticoats. "It isn't like Simone to be late."

"She wouldn't miss this day for anything," Charlotte reassured her.

"If Elliot had lived, Simone would be Mistress of Wyngate instead of me."

"Don't be thinking unhappy thoughts, darling. We can't bring back the past. I don't think it matters to Simone. She's happy on her ranch in the valley. You should start getting ready. I must go downstairs and consult with Hannah."

Doing as her grandmother asked, Adrienne let her unhappy thoughts fade away and began to dress. Today, she wore her dark wavy hair down to her shoulders. Her midnight blue eyes and tall, statuesque figure came from the Wyngates.

Smiling, Simone entered the room. "Sorry I'm late. I was halfway here when the Jeep acted up again."

Adrienne reached out and took her dearest friend in her arms, pulling her close. Tears came to her eyes. They hugged, and then Simone pulled away.

"This is your day, darling. If Elliot were alive, he wouldn't like to see you acting this way. His dying in that car accident is God's way of telling us to make each day count. Now, let's get you dressed."

When Simone finished helping Adrienne, she looked as if she had stepped from the pages of a bridal magazine. She stood before the full-length mirror and admired the beautiful image standing before her. The lace mantilla added to the beauty of it all.

"You look absolutely gorgeous, my friend."

Adrienne turned and smiled. Simone's dark hair and voluptuous body caught many men's eye. Today, she looked especially lovely in lavender silk. After Elliot's death, she never seemed to notice the way men looked at her. She deserved all the happiness that came her way.

They left Adrienne's room and walked down the hall to the top of the stairs. Adrienne looked around, but didn't see her ancestors anywhere and wondered why. She knew they wouldn't want to miss her special day.

"When I decide to marry," Simone said, "I'll have Royce do my flowers. He's done a wonderful job for you."

Soft, lilting music, laughter and the murmur of conversations floated up from the ballroom below. Adrienne and Simone waited for the wedding march to begin. They would walk down the stairs to meet Alex, and he would escort Adrienne into the ballroom. She picked at the pearls on her gown. She wasn't the nervous type, but today her anticipation and excitement showed. Everyone around her sounded happy.

Behind Adrienne, Simone fidgeted with the flowing detachable train. Adrienne smiled at her and said nothing, knowing it would fall into place when she descended the long spiral staircase. Was every bride this nervous on her wedding day?

"Stop wiggling and be still or I'll have to readjust your train all over again," urged Simone.

Adrienne had a good view of the foyer below. She was surprised to see Peter Llewellyn, Steven's best man, approach Charlotte and Alex, her brother-in-law. He handed Alex a note. Her grandmother stood waiting. Alex handed the note to Charlotte. She saw him take Charlotte aside and whisper to her. Adrienne watched with mounting fear that Hannah's prediction was about to come true.

"Something's wrong." Her voice was just above a whisper. In her soul, she had a feeling she couldn't shake. Her heart beat faster. She started down the stairs, but Simone held her back.

"Wait. Don't go until we find out what they have to say."

"Something's happened to Steven." Adrienne grew cold with fear.

"How do you know?" Simone demanded.

"I have this awful feeling in the pit of my stomach." Dread replaced the happiness she felt a few minutes ago. She put her hand over her mouth to stop from crying.

Two faces as white as the ribbons that lined the staircase looked up at her. Charlotte and Alex ascended the stairs and approached her. From where she stood, she saw tears on her grandmother's cheeks. Alex smoldered with anger. He whispered something to Charlotte. She placed a gentle hand on his arm.

Adrienne watched in agitated dismay as they neared. Her heart stopped. Chills of fear ran down her spine. Once they reached the top of the stairs, Adrienne could wait no longer.

"What's happened?"

They didn't answer immediately.

Then, Charlotte spoke in a faltering voice. "This note is for you."

With unsteady hands, Adrienne handed Simone her bouquet and felt her blood turn to slivers of ice. She accepted the note from Charlotte. A feeling of detachment she couldn't explain came over her. Her heart raced, and she thought it would fly out of her chest. Her hands trembled as she opened the note and read it aloud.

"Adrienne, I can't marry you. I'm still in love with Margo. I'm returning to the States. Steven."

Adrienne stood dumbfounded. The note didn't sound like Steven and neither did the writing look like his. It was similar, but not Steven's. Last night there wasn't a hint of unhappiness in their phone conversation. He told her how much he loved her and couldn't wait for today when they would become man and wife."

Her heart cried out that the note was a lie. She'd been overjoyed in her happiness. Had she missed something in Steven's voice or his actions? Someone was playing a cruel joke. The note told her a different story. Steven wasn't here.

"I'm so sorry, my dear." Charlotte took her granddaughter in her arms. Adrienne wanted to cry but couldn't, and pulled away from Charlotte's arms.

Alex was like a big brother to her. She saw the sadness in his eyes as he spoke. "This is not like the Steven I know. I'll send Trinidad and some of my men to find him." His sympathy for her heartache was obvious.

Feeling faint, she leaned against Simone, who wrapped her arms around her. A few tears escaped her.

"Simone, please put my bouquet on the chest."

"Here, take my handkerchief," Simone prompted. Adrienne wiped her eyes.

"What are you going to do?" Charlotte's sadness showed.

Adrienne hesitated before speaking. "I'll give you my answer when I enter the ballroom."

No one said anything. She wasn't about to cower and hide in her room. The stillness around her was explosive. She struggled to fight her tears and gulped for breath. She looked at Charlotte and Simone.

"I'm a Wyngate. Like all the Wyngates before me, I stand tall in the face of adversity."

Peter, her childhood friend, and Steven's best man, stood alone, watching. She saw the sadness in his eyes. Simone was silent.

Charlotte held her hand and with the other one wiped tears from her face with a delicate lace handkerchief.

Alex waited for her to regain her composure. All the people she cared about were here except the most important one, Steven.

"I'm so sorry."

Alex took her hands, and her heart went out to him. She sensed his sadness.

"Would you like me to inform the guests?"

"Thank you for offering, Alex, but it's only right I do it. This was to be my wedding day." Her voice grew steadier as she spoke. "I am a Wyngate. No matter how difficult it is, the Wyngates are fighters." She paused a moment, seeking control.

"Damn, it hurts." She closed her eyes to hold back the tears. After a moment, she opened her eyes, determined to see the reception through.

Releasing Alex's hands, she moved away, her head high. She wouldn't break down and yield to heartache. Later, when she was alone, the pain and the tears would come, but for now, she would stay strong.

"Wyngates are all that," Alex agreed. "I'll find Trinidad and see what he's discovered."

"We'll get through this together." Simone patted her arm.

Adrienne stiffened her back and led the way to the staircase.

What would her guests say when they learned the richest woman in the islands had been jilted on her wedding day? It didn't matter. It was plain enough to see. With her head held steady and a fixed smile on her face, she took Alex's arm, slowly descended the stairway, and entered the ballroom.

At a signal from Alex, the musicians ceased playing. Whispered conversations stopped. People turned and stared at Adrienne as she walked down the long white carpeted aisle. Her gown's train flowed majestically behind her as her grandmother and Simone followed.

Murmurs of concern and dismay rose from the guests. All faces followed her until she reached the front of the room. She turned and clapped her hands twice in the island tradition to gain her guests' attention. Stillness settled over those present.

With her smile in place and her voice as normal as she could make it, she began to speak. "Ladies and gentlemen, there will be no wedding ceremony today."

She did not explain. The news would be all over the island within the hour. The outside world would learn the details of her rejection soon enough. Shock and disbelief showed on the faces of her guests.

"Please bear with me in this difficult time," Adrienne continued over the murmur of their voices.

Her vision blurred as she fought back tears. Her pain was unbearable, but her pride was stronger.

"Many of you came a long distance for this festive day. There's no reason why the celebration shouldn't continue. There's plenty of food and wine. Please, everyone, enjoy yourselves. Eat, drink, and be merry."

Alex took over when Adrienne stopped. "My grandfather use to say, make the most of the party, especially when someone else is paying for it."

His little speech broke the ice. He nodded to the orchestra and they swung into a lively tune. Waiters circled the room and made sure every guest had champagne. At some of the tables, people gathered in small groups gossiping and wondering what really happened. Others joined in the celebration. All that mattered to Adrienne was for her guests to have a good time. She mingled with them, danced, and drank champagne.

Adrienne was a sad queen with all her subjects in attendance, except the King. She was never without a partner. Peter danced with her several times.

"I'm sorry, my love. Steven's a damn fool for leaving you. You know I love you. I'll always be around if you need me."

"Thank you, Peter. You've always been a good friend."

Later, Alex came and danced with her again. Strong and solid, Alex held her. It felt good having his arms around her for support. He'd always been there to protect her, but he couldn't protect her from a broken heart.

He leaned down and whispered in her ear. "You're definitely a

Wyngate, my dear. Your folks would have been proud of you."

Adrienne tried to think of something witty to say, but nothing came to mind.

"You're as beautiful as my Aimee was."

"After all these years, you still miss her?"

"Yes, I do." He grinned as he twirled her around the room.

Adrienne never stopped smiling because if she did, everyone would see her wounded heart. She had built an image of self-assurance and stableness. All of it would come tumbling down if she relaxed. She danced with old friends and quickly lost track of time.

Chapter Five

It was growing late when a gentleman Adrienne didn't recognize entered the room and caused a stir among her guests. She watched as he made his way toward her and cut in on her dance partner. He didn't introduce himself, and she was too weary to ask. He swept her into his arms and glided with her across the floor. The touch of the stranger's hand on her waist and shoulder reminded her of someone. She blamed it on the lingering effects of Steven's rejection and the champagne. She'd told herself, she'd had more than enough to drink.

Adrienne pulled back and looked into the stranger's face. It startled her. Liquid gold eyes stared at her under dark, silver streaked hair and lashes. His hair was fashionably cut.

She gazed into the face of a handsome older man. He was well preserved and old enough to be her father, a man who could set a room full of people abuzz with curiosity. In his late sixties, he appeared a man of intrigue and mystery.

She leaned forward and rested her head on his shoulder. She felt safe and comfortable in his arms. He didn't seem to mind. She felt so tired. It was nice having someone to lean on. A sense of loss and sorrow welled inside her.

The stranger whirled her around the dance floor several times to an old-fashioned waltz. He watched her like an artist admiring a masterpiece. The swaying movements of her body were captured in his eyes. People stopped to watch and ask questions of others, curious to know who the newcomer was. Adrienne didn't care.

She had lifted her head, and he watched her in appreciation through narrowed lids for a long time without speaking. When he did, his voice

18

was smooth as the rum her family sold for generations.

"I'm sorry. I missed the ceremony. You make a beautiful bride. I haven't seen the groom. Where is Steven?"

"How dare you mention Steven," Adrienne's voice rose in shock.

By this time, the other guests had stopped dancing and watched with interest as the scene unfolded before them. Her smile disappeared. Every muscle in her face froze.

"There was no ceremony," she said in a low voice laced with anger.

The stranger took her by the shoulders and stared into her eyes. She tried to shake him off, but he held her too tightly.

"What do you mean there was no ceremony? Where is Steven?" The harshness in his voice upset her.

"You weren't here when I made the announcement." She threw her words at him.

"What announcement?" His eyes glittered like a tiger about to strike.

"The groom sent me a note. He decided he had some unfinished business in the States." Her voice broke, and embarrassment flushed her face.

The man dropped his hands. "Steven would never do a thing like that."

His face became cold and unseeing. Without another word, he turned and left her standing alone in the middle of the dance floor.

Puzzled by the man and his unceremonious departure, Adrienne was left pondering this new turn of events. Something was terribly wrong.

Her grandmother, Alex, and Simone rushed over to her. "Who was that man?" they demanded

"I haven't the slightest idea. When I told him there was no ceremony and Steven had returned to the States, he became upset."

Filled with grief, it was a struggle to keep from breaking down in front of her guests. Peter wrapped his arms around her and pulled her head to his shoulder.

"I'm sure everything will be alright."

Looking into Peter's kind eyes, she wondered why she hadn't been able to fall in love with him. She gently pulled away from him.

"Thank you, Peter, you're a true friend."

"Any time, my love."

"How did the stranger get in?" Her grandmother looked puzzled.

"I'll check to see if he had an invitation," Alex offered and left.

"He must have had an invitation. Do you know his name?" Peter said.

"I didn't recognize him. It doesn't matter."

Deep inside, despite the man's reaction, Adrienne felt drawn to the stranger and wondered if she would see him again. She had no idea why.

"It isn't every day a woman has the honor of being jilted by two handsome men," she said.

Chapter Six

Adrienne sighed with relief when the last guests departed. She had stood her ground and showed them what it was to be a Wyngate. It hadn't been easy. She knew her grandmother was proud of her for doing what she did.

"Adrienne, would you like Peter and me to stay? We don't want to leave you alone." Simone's offer sounded odd to Adrienne because Simone and Peter had never been close. She hoped they were trying to turn their dislike for each other into something positive.

"Go." Even her close friends were unwelcome this evening.

"Are you sure?" Simone looked concerned. "It's not good for you to be alone."

"Let us stay," Peter insisted.

"Please go. I just want Alex and Charlotte. I'll be fine."

An idea began forming. After Simone and Peter left, Adrienne, her grandmother, and Alex returned to the ballroom. She informed them of her plans.

"Everything is to stay just the way it is."

Mortified, Charlotte protested. "Leave everything the way it is?"

"Yes. Everything is to remain as it is at this moment. No presents will be returned. The tables with their settings and flowers are to stay exactly as they are. Nothing is to be cleaned or removed from this room. When I leave here tonight, Wyngate by the Sea will be closed and locked until I decide otherwise."

With eyes bright with suppressed tears, Adrienne continued, "Everything will be left as it is. It will be a reminder that happiness for a Wyngate is only an illusion."

"Adrienne, I know it's been difficult, but..."

"I'm sorry, Grandmother, that's the way I want it." She could tell Alex didn't like her orders either.

"You know what will happen. The mice will have a field day," Charlotte said.

"Let them."

"Adrienne, this is not wise." Alex took her hand in his.

"I know, but it's the way I want it."

"Will nothing make you change your mind?"

"No." Her voice held a tinge of sharpness. "Send the caterers and the servants home. They're no longer needed. Alex, will you take my grandmother home? She's overtired from all the excitement and needs to rest."

"Of course, it's always a pleasure. It's been a difficult day for you," Alex said.

"I'm fine. I'll stay here with you," Charlotte insisted.

"Please go with Alex. I need time to be alone and think." Adrienne hugged her grandmother. "I love you. Don't worry, I won't be late."

Alex seemed unsure of her state of mind. "Adrienne, I don't like this."

"You needn't worry. I won't do anything foolish. I promise I'll be back at the cottage before midnight."

"I still don't like it," Alex grumbled.

"Just go. I'll be fine." Despite the worry on Charlotte's face, she urged them to leave.

After they left, Adrienne climbed the stairs to her room, unable to hold back her tears any longer. She didn't try to stop them, and let them flow down her cheeks and onto her wedding gown. She shut out the evening noises and listened only to the sea wash against the shore. She kicked off her shoes and flounced on her bed. She had a long cry, exhausting herself of all emotion. Without meaning to, she slept.

She awakened to the creaking noises of her room. She had never grown used to the sounds. Were her ancestors complaining about her decision to leave everything the way it was? It didn't matter what they thought. They had no say in what she did or didn't do with her home. They were ghosts of the past and Sir John and the Contessa would understand.

Adrienne had been careful of how much champagne she drank, yet her head throbbed to the beat of native drums. She got up, the lace on her wedding gown whispered in the darkness. She fumbled to undo the buttons and pulled the soft material away from her body, leaving it in a pile on the floor. Reconsidering, she reached down, carefully picked it up, and hung it on its satin hanger. Taking off her petticoats, she put them on the bed. From her closet, she picked out a full-length cotton gown and slipped into it, adding sandals to her feet.

How long had she slept? In the semi-darkness, she moved over to her bureau and turned on the lamp. Through puffy eyes, she squinted at the clock. It was eleven o'clock. Her gaze came to rest on the gold and white engraved wedding invitation. She picked it up and for a moment, lovingly caressed it. Then, with all the fury of a woman scorned, she tore it up and let the pieces scatter across the floor.

Adrienne's heartache and pain were taking a greater toll on her then she expected. She took her bridal bouquet off her grandfather's sea chest and threw it hard against the wall marring and crushing the delicate blooms. Fury rising, she threw her mantilla to the floor and stomped on it, tearing it apart. Ivory, lace, and pearls crunched under her feet. Adrienne screamed and screamed, releasing all her anger. The sound echoed through the empty room, bouncing off the walls and ceiling.

She let her temper and frustrations run their course. It had a healing effect. Now, she could go on. Instead of being married, she was a woman scorned. A Wyngate left at the altar was something unheard of. It would give the tabloids and the locals enough gossip to chew on for weeks.

A little setback like this never kept a Wyngate down. The pain and the knowing looks would hurt for a while, but she'd survive. She went into her bathroom, took two aspirins from a bottle, and gulped them down with a full glass of water. She hoped to ward off the headache she felt building behind her eyes. Like the thunder she heard in the distance, the storm would come soon.

When she left her room, instead of going downstairs, she headed down the unlit hallway to the Great Hall to see Sir John and Theo. She knew exactly how many steps it would take to get to the end of the carpeted hall and the doors to the gallery. As a little girl, she had memorized them. It had been a good place to sit and think after she had gotten in trouble for some minor infraction. When she came to the end, she reached out, opened the doors, and turned on the lights. Overhead lights flooded the two brightly lit paintings at the end of the hall.

According to history, Johnnie was born with the title. As a pirate, he was never a gentleman. Sir John had already captured his enemy's armada. Stealing their ships and gold wasn't enough. He also stole the Captain's wife, the Contessa Theodora, who became his lover and later his wife. They settled on Santa Isabella, and she gave him two sons.

The house they lived in was built by Sir John from his own plans.

A notorious pirate known as Bloody Bertie Llewellyn, tried to capture Sir John's ships, but he was never successful. Sir John was too smart. The feud between the Llewellyns and the Wyngates continued for several generations. After many years, the feud was forgotten and the families became friends.

Laws, Conduct of the Court, and the world never mattered to Sir John. Throughout his infamous career, he made his own rules. He used Theo's gold and her fallen woman status to keep her in line. No one had discovered what happened to the gold. Sir John was supposed to have won it at cards and buried it on the estate. From that day on, it was referred to as the Dead Man's Gold.

Adrienne saw the disgruntled look on Johnnie's face and the Contessa's sympathetic smile.

"Damn you both. Why couldn't you have been happy with what you had and left the rest of us out of your shenanigans?"

'We cannot foresee the future.'

She reached out to turn off the lights. For a moment, she imagined she heard a voice.

'As long as there is a Wyngate...'

All else was lost in the loud rumbling of thunder. It shook the house, making Adrienne jump. She tried not to let the threatening storm bother her already strained nerves and quickly made her way back to the main hall. Lightning brightened her way down the long hallway. She leaned on the banister for support. She touched the drooping flowers along the banister. The wall sconces, still gave off dim light as wavering shadows formed eerie patterns on the walls.

Wyngate Manor

Darkness hid in corners where the dim light couldn't reach. Not for the first time, she felt eyes watching her. It was something she felt many times in the old house.

She had lived here all of her life. No one had access to any of the hidden passages and storerooms in the cliffs below the house. Her grandfather had sealed them off after she had gotten lost in them when she was a little girl.

Shadows hid in the far recesses of the house with faces and eyes she couldn't see. Wyngate-by-the-Sea had a heartbeat of its own only she could hear. The stillness would unnerve the stoutest of souls. She'd once loved it, but she wasn't sure about anything anymore. Leaving it might be a good idea. It was something she would think about.

Chapter Seven

The heavy humidity from the open windows brought dampness. It settled around Adrienne like a cloying perfume. A strong breeze ruffled the draperies. The storm would come, and she would relish every minute of its fury.

Entering the ballroom, she turned the lights on and looked at the scene before her. There was little of the beautiful wedding cake left but dried up crumbs. Some chairs were pushed back from the tables set with the family's finest china and crystal. It looked as though something had disturbed her guests and they had left in a hurry. Not a dish or plate had been removed. It would stay that way. The room looked lonely and forlorn. It reminded her of a girl dressed for the ball and all that remained afterward was a tired old woman.

Charlotte and Alex accepted her wishes to be alone. Trinidad had disappeared at Alex's request to find out what he could about Steven's departure. Having known Trinidad all her life, she knew his dark eyes revealed nothing of his feelings. He was torn between two worlds that of the white man and that of his island ancestors. It hasn't been easy for him. His family included a long line of medicine men and woman, in the tribes native to the island. Some still held to the old beliefs of Voodoo with its spirits and magic. Secrets and suspicions were hidden from the outside world. His Christian upbringing clashed with that of his family, yet he fit in both worlds and, like every islander, had secrets of his own. If any answers existed, he would find them and report to Alex.

She faltered and leaned against a table for support. The crystal on it tingled in the stillness. The heartbreaking note from Steven had changed everything. Earlier, he had said he had broken with his fiancé months before he met Adrienne, and it was by mutual agreement. She had valued her independence too much to share their life together or have a family.

Maybe, Adrienne hadn't known Steven as well as she thought. Had he been lying to her all this time? Had he been truthful in telling her about his engagement? He said he wanted children and a family and his ex-girlfriend didn't. Her career was more important.

In love, Adrienne probably should have paid more attention to the things Steven said. It didn't matter now. She had to pick up the pieces and go on with her life. Maybe in years to come she would understand and be able to forgive him for causing her such heartache.

Why was the stranger tonight so upset when she told him about Steven? He'd evidently known him. There were many questions she wanted answered. It was just another oddity to add to this bewildering day.

Adrienne ignored the wedding gifts that lined the Madeira lace covered tables at the side of the room.

She knew her grandmother hadn't been pleased with her decision. Charlotte came from the old school of etiquette where things were done by the book. Against her better judgment, Charlotte would carry out Adrienne's wishes. Maybe she didn't agree with her plan, but she understood her heartbreak.

It was Adrienne's home to do with as she pleased, and this was what she wanted. Her ancestors would turn over in their graves in protest of her lack of manners in not returning the wedding gifts and sending notes of regret. Perhaps only Sir John and the Contessa would understand her actions. Others would never forgive her for leaving her beautiful house abandoned and in a state of disarray.

She stepped through an open window onto the terrace. A moisture-laden breeze drifted up the cliffs from the sea below. The moon appeared momentarily from behind dark blue clouds and cast its silver radiance far out to sea. She was drawn to it as if in a trance. What would it be like to follow that ethereal staircase into eternal peace with her ancestors? The thought quickly slipped from her mind. It wasn't her way or her forefather's before her. She wasn't going to give in at the first sign of disappointment. Whether married or single, she would go on.

A star-studded sky and a moon as bright as a new gold piece now shone above her. Why? She didn't know. Maybe after hundreds of years, it wanted someone to love it.

The stars were swallowed by the rapidly approaching storm clouds, and the sky darkened. Clouds scurried across the moon, hiding it. The squall hit fast and furious. The wind, cold and ruthless, tugged at her gown. Lightning streaked across the skies and thunder rumbled ominously through the heavens. The wind increased as pelting rain beat against the shutters of the house. She felt nothing.

The wind whipped the curtains into a frenzy of chaotic movement through the open windows. Lawn furniture slid and tumbled. She stood there unmoving against the storm, oblivious to the chaos around her. Adrienne didn't see or recognize anything.

She left the terrace and fought her way down the overgrown path with its dense plants and flora to the beach. She didn't know why getting to the beach was important. The leaves and vines of all shapes and sizes with darkened colors sought to entangle her. At the beach, her sandals sank into the wet sand, slowing her way. Finally, she left them behind in her tracks.

Palm trees bowed to Mother Nature's fury. The storm was stronger here, and Adrienne watched silently as it tossed gigantic waves against the shore, only to recede and push forward time and time again in its never-ending battle to stake its claim.

Far out on the coral strand, a flash of lightning etched against the dark sky. The ghostly image of The Virginia Lady, shipwrecked more than seventy years ago, lay stranded. Her broken masts stood high out of the water. A shattered hull could still be seen at low tide. The hull was ravaged by the relentless sea never letting go of its hold on land.

Through the storm, Adrienne stood entranced by its majestic beauty. Her rain soaked hair lay plastered to the sides of her face and neck. Her cotton gown clung to her wet shivering body. Yet, she didn't move. Now, more than anything, she knew she wouldn't give up. She would fight her battles and win.

"Adrienne, Adrienne." Her name sounded in the night. It carried over the wind as more torrential rains battered her body.

She put her hands up to cover her ears and shut out the beckoning voice. Then the storm ended as suddenly as it had begun with a silence that overwhelmed. The moon appeared above the dark clouds. Adrienne swayed to the rhythm of the sighing palms. Again, she heard her name.

"Adrienne."

She turned and saw Steven in his white tux silhouetted against the trees a few feet away.

With outstretched arms, he called to her. "Darling, come to me."

She struggled to move. She reached out to him. "Steven, help me."

When he came closer, she tried to wrap her arms around him, only to see him fade away. She held nothing in her arms.

Engrossed in her fantasy, she didn't hear the stranger approach her from behind and put his arms around her. She turned in his arms believing it was Steven, but, all she saw was a man in black, wearing dark gloves and a weird mask was covering his face.

"Who are you? What do you want?" She fought to loosen his grip, but the man was too strong.

"It is you I want, my dear Adrienne."

Adrienne didn't like what was happening and tried to free herself from the man's grip only finding she was suffocating. She twisted and turned, struggling to escape him. Then, he hit her on the jaw, knocking her unconscious.

She felt herself being dragged to the shoreline. The tide was coming in, and the cool water, splashed over her body as he dragged her farther into the surf. She regained consciousness and lifted her head. She heard voices and saw lanterns approaching in the distance. The man suddenly released her and ran for the forest, leaving her half drowned. With all her strength, she clawed her way from the surf onto solid ground. That was where Trinidad and his men found her.

The next thing she remembered was being in the hospital. The police asked her what had happened, but she could tell them nothing other than going to the beach. She couldn't remember.

Three weeks later, she left her island home for the mainland.

Chapter Eight

The island of St. Claire

The Order of the Blue Sisters of Mercy, were excited to have a guest. It was amusing to see five old ladies vying for one man's attention. He wasn't an easy man to tend. They did what they could for the badly beaten patient.

It was not like the old days, when the hospital was a Leper Colony and there was little known about the disease. Then, they had patients. The Sisters always had a heavy workload and plenty of help. After the Diocese closed the hospital, there were no doctors, nurses, or patients left, only the sisters

The sisters who stayed behind had known no life other then administering to the sick. They were old and too afraid to enter the outside world. To go into a home would upset their daily routine. The sisters were pensioned off and allowed to stay on the island.

The sisters had given their lives to helping the sick. It had been five years since the church and the hospital closed. A boat came once a week from the mainland with supplies and attended to their daily needs. Now a stranger had joined them.

Sister Theresa now knew who he was. It didn't matter. They worked night and day to save him. If they had modern facilities, they could have done more.

Steven Forrester watched the sisters flitter about him. The women were like doting relatives. They waited on him as though he were the Bishop himself. His condition had improved in the month he was there. They wanted to make him comfortable. He gave Sister Josephina the information she needed to contact his Uncle Charles.

They were enjoying his company before Charlie came for him. He would need reconstructive surgery. The injuries to his face hadn't healed properly. They wanted to make sure he was well enough to make the trip to the hospital in Miami.

Uncle Charlie arrived a week later. Steven was airlifted by helicopter to a private hospital. It was the last they saw of him.

A few weeks later, carpenters and electricians under Charlie's supervision arrived on the island. They renovated the sister's quarters and repaired whatever needed fixing, compliments of their uninvited guest.

Chapter Nine

Three Years Later

Adrienne's flight home was nearing its end. The plane approached the big island. In the distance, she could see the lights of Santa Isabella. A frisson of happiness and anticipation engulfed her.

A serious bout with pneumonia after her wedding disaster weakened Adrienne, and she left her island paradise soon after. She intended to stay away until the wounds of rejection healed. Now, she was returning to a world she no longer knew.

It wasn't often that a wealthy young woman was left standing at the altar in front of one-hundred and fifty guests. Her good friend, Peter, had stood by her in those difficult days. They had been friends since childhood. They were more like brother and sister. She wondered if he had found someone else to love. Was he happy?

The past was behind her. The future lay ahead. News of her arrival would be all over the island by morning. The native telegraph was far more efficient than the telephone. Her grandmother would be happy to see her, but it would have to wait until tomorrow. Charlotte never liked her sleep interrupted at such a late hour.

Uneasiness disturbed Adrienne. Why was she so edgy? She was coming home to the people and places she loved. She thought about her home and the legend of the Dead Man's Gold, supposedly buried somewhere on her estate by the family's founder, the pirate, Sir John Wyngate.

She had been content with her former lifestyle. She had gone to all the parties and social affairs she was required to attend as the islands most prosperous rum maker. She had enjoyed working in the mill to help produce the 'Dead Man's Gold Rum'. Through the years, the business had made her family millionaires.

At twenty-six, she had developed an inner confidence, was stronger, and able to face her future. She had no financial worries when it came to money or the family business. Wyngate Industries were run by some of the smartest men in the business. Thorough audits were conducted each year to assure Wyngate was sound and profitable for her and her employees.

Steven's disappearance was never solved, even with Alex's connections. They had no idea what happened to him.

She hailed a taxi to take her across town to the ferry. She started to get in the cab when a man stopped her.

"I hope you don't mind if I join you. I'm catching the ferry to Santa Isabella and don't want to miss it." He had a scar running down the right side of his face, and his smile intrigued her.

"I don't mind sharing the cab."

Adrienne didn't want to refuse the man. He looked like a modern day pirate with dark hair streaked with gray. He must have been in a terrible accident.

"Are you visiting Santa Isabella," she asked as he helped her into the cab.

"I live there," he replied.

"Oh." He must be new to the island. She was curious.

"I've lived there for eighteen-months. I brought Hunter's Lodge." He smiled at her.

"It's been deserted for years."

"It was in bad shape. My partner and I renovated it."

"I'm glad you bought it. I hate to see old houses destroyed and replaced by modern homes and condos."

He smiled again. Her words had pleased him. At the ferry landing, he helped her out of the cab. She reached in her bag to pay the cabbie when he stopped her.

"Put your money away, Miss Wyngate. You were kind enough to share your cab."

"You know who I am, but, I don't know who you are."

"Tyler Prescott, I'm a land developer. I buy up old estates.

Sometimes I remodel them, and sometimes they have to be torn down. It depends on their condition. If there is land, it makes the project more challenging."

Adrienne had to stop and think before she answered. "That's very interesting." Was he looking to buy Wyngate? It was the largest property on the island.

"Let me carry your bag." He took the bag from her with his good arm.

Inside the terminal, the ticket line for the ferry started to move. Adrienne bent over to pick up her bag where Tyler had put it at her feet. She straightened up and inadvertently elbowed him.

"I'm sorry." She smiled an apology.

"It's quite all right. I'm glad it wasn't your bag."

Adrienne's gaze came in contact with the most intelligent hazel eyes. The scar took nothing away from his good looks. She could tell his tanned skin was from being out in the sun for long hours at a time. His smile alone would melt any woman's heart. Somehow, she had the feeling his smile was just for her. The nearness of the man quickened her pulse.

Adrienne hadn't been interested in any man since she was jilted. It was ridiculous. He was a complete stranger. While standing in line, he handed her a business card with his name and address on it.

"Thank you, I'll keep your card in case I ever decide to sell Wyngate." She read the card out loud. "Tyler Prescott and Associates, Land Development, Construction and Appraisals."

"I'm not interested in Wyngate." His facial expression was intriguing to watch.

"If not Wyngate, what are you interested in Mr. Prescott?"

"I'm interested in only you."

She couldn't believe what he said. "We've just met. You don't know anything about me." She frowned.

"Not at this moment, but I will." He moved away. His words remained.

The sight of the big bright red and white hull of the ferryboat put her in a festive mood. Its huge belly swallowed cars, cargo, and passengers alike. It swayed gently against the pilings in the evening tide. Her engines were idling to let the cars and passengers disembark. Then, she joined the waiting cars and passengers boarding the ferry's cavernous accommodations. She was tired and sought out a quiet spot to wait.

Her thoughts turned to Tyler Prescott. Was he coming home for business or pleasure? Whoever he was, he fitted these surroundings.

It had been a long time since Adrienne had met such an intriguing man. She had stopped comparing men to Steven long ago. Something about Tyler reminded her of Steven. She turned to look for him. He was standing a few feet away from her and returned her smile. Slightly embarrassed at being caught looking, she quickly took her book out of her carryall to read. She evidently met with his approval because she could still feel his gaze upon her.

His imperfections didn't bother her. He seemed to have adjusted to his situation. She looked back.

His gaze was intense. It made her edgy, like a young girl caught flirting. He was an attractive man with a commanding presence. Yet, there was a sad look about him as he turned and walked away. His limp was more noticeable. Even without it, he was a man who would stand out wherever he went.

Tourists and natives filled the lounge. Restless, she headed forward toward the bow of the ship to feel the evening breezes. She found a seat and stowed her carryall underneath it. She drew out her well-worn paperback mystery and resumed reading. After a few minutes, she gave up trying and put her book away. The overhead lights kept blinking on and off. The sun was beginning to set.

She went over and leaned against the rail, letting the breeze soothe her. A thought ran through her mind. Did Jolie still have a liking for Romantic Suspense?

The stranger's face replaced her old friend in her thoughts. She had never met him before. No woman would forget a man like him. She gave up and went inside.

There, passengers milled about. A small bar occupied the one end of the lounge. Soon the ship's horn announced their departure. The trip to the island of Santa Isabella took forty minutes and then another ten to fifteen minutes for the ferry to unload the cars and passengers. It was then ten more minutes to the family owned hotel. She thought of home and the word sounded strange.

The lounge grew hot and stuffy. Why was she so restless?

Again, she found herself outside. She breathed in the salty night air. The turquoise green sea had darkened and lapped against the ship's hull. The ferry slowly made its way out of the channel and into the open sea. Too keyed up to think about anything, she walked around the deck. Salty mists of seawater sprayed her face, blowing her shoulder length hair into disarray. It felt good coming home, didn't it?

It would take time to adjust to the island's tempo. Like most other Caribbean Islands, nothing was hurried. Time was something she had in abundance. She'd go slow and take it easy, she promised herself. Darkness crept around her like a suffocating blanket.

Fragments of conversation reached her. People stood in groups talking, laughing, and relating their latest adventures to their newfound friends. She was alone and shivered as the cool sea breeze increased. She turned to see Tyler watching her.

"It's gotten quite cool this evening," he remarked.

She knew she had to be polite. "I don't remember the nights being this chilly."

"Are you returning home?"

"I left some time ago." Adrienne replied. Talking with him was easy and she found she wanted to talk to him. It had been so long since she had a conversation with an interesting man. She had avoided relationships for the past three years.

"Now, you're coming home," he said in a friendly tone.

"Yes, I'm coming home."

She wasn't sure how it sounded. It didn't matter. She was happy. They lapsed into silence. The lights outside the lounge had stopped flickering and reflected off his strong face. Again, he reminded her of Steven. She scolded herself for remembering him. She had tried so hard to forget.

"It's nice talking to you," Adrienne said softly.

"Thank you. Have a pleasant homecoming."

She watched him turn and walk away. She already missed the feeling of his warmth. She pulled her light jacket closer and hurried inside. Trying to avoid a waiter, she bumped into Tyler again, and dropped her bag. She bent down to pick up what had fallen out. He too bent down and their eyes met. A feeling of contentment settled over her.

Why did he affect her this way? They had talked once in the taxi and again here on the ferry. He awakened feelings she'd buried with Steven's departure. A wide grin dazzled her. His eyes were caressing her. It almost undid her.

"It hasn't been a good day, has it? he said knowingly.

"I've had better days," she agreed.

"I hope nothing is missing." He handed her the bag and smiled.

She rummaged through the contents. "Everything seems to be here."

"Good. We keep bumping into each other. Would you like to join me for a drink?"

"That's not necessary." Having a drink with this man would lead to other things, things she didn't want and couldn't handle at this time. Part of her wanted to say yes, the other part of her wanted to say no. "It's very kind of you, but no thanks." She refused to yield to her feelings.

Abruptly turning, she left before he could change her mind. It had nothing to do with his disabilities. He wasn't that old. Something about the man bothered her. Was she still afraid of making another bad choice? Any other woman would have jumped at his offer.

In the overcrowded lounge, she found herself a seat at a small table by the door. The lemonade she got at the bar was cool and refreshing. She looked up, and her gaze met his. He openly stared at her from across the room.

She wore a crumpled slack suit that had seen better days. She could use a bath and some pampering at Dana's Salon, if she was still in Old Town. There were many other attractive women on board. Why had he picked her?

She was a Wyngate. Was that that the reason he was so interested?"

The ferry's horns sounded their arrival at the wharf in Santa Isabella. The ship pushed its bulk into a slip, battering the pilings as it went. Cars and trucks were unloaded first, then the passengers.

Waiting to cross the square, she was surprised to see Tyler talking to a tall heavyset islander. Trinidad's teeth shined like a string of pearls in the night. She'd known that smile all her life. He was her brother-in-law Alex's right-hand man. They were talking like they were old friends.

Trinidad's face showed no surprise at seeing Adrienne. It was as if he was used to seeing her get off the ferry. How many other people knew she was coming home? Soon the whole island would know.

Was Tyler a friend of Alex's? Was it business or personal? She doubted Alex was in any trouble. Avalon, Alex's casino, had been in his family for more generations than she could remember.

Alex had married Aimee, her older sister. A hit and run driver killed Aimee and her unborn child. The car had been abandoned and the driver was never found.

Curious, she watched the two men drive off in a jeep toward the other end of the island where the casino was located. It left her with many unanswered questions. The only way to get the answers was to see her old friend Jolie. She'd know all about Tyler Prescott's presence on the island and what he was doing.

Chapter Ten

Adrienne watched the jeep's taillights disappear along Shore Drive and continue away from town. A merry assortment of tourists and shoppers mingled in the square. Across the square, a group of sailors enjoyed a night of fun. The island was a routine port of call for Navy ships. Belle Town was the closest they came to a large city where they could relax and enjoy themselves.

The island never seemed to shut down, and the tourists were making the most of their visit. Music and laughter flowed from the First and Last Chance Café. Adrienne, now rejuvenated, decided to join the festivities.

Several times, she found herself greeted by a boisterous group of people asking her to join them, but she refused. In the middle of the square, she looked around and raised her arms.

"It's good to be home," she shouted. No one paid any attention to her.

She made it to Jolie's Café before too many people blocked her way. Inside, a bar lined one wall while in a corner a band played to a group of dancing people. The loud lively music encouraged young people to gyrate to the latest music by one of the island's hip-hop groups.

Adrienne pressed her way through the throng of people and left the main room for the more sedate lounge. The sound of soft lilting piano music floating around the room greeted her. In the semi-darkness, she stood watching and listening to Norman, Jolie's, son, playing the piano. Music had been his passion since he was in his teens.

Four years older than Adrienne, he wore his clothes with a flare only he could manage. Broad shoulders and brownish blonde hair curling just above the collar of his jacket added to his good looks. Tall, he would have many female followers if he weren't married.

He looked up and smiled at her. "I've missed you."

"Thank you. It's been too long," she replied as she leaned on the top of the piano. A smile replaced her uneasiness. "How is the family?"

"Fiona and I are doing well. Our family has grown since you went away. Leslie is four and Randy is one."

"How is Jolie?"

"With Mom, it's still the status quo. She likes her independence and takes a vacation once in awhile. Not for long. She doesn't trust anyone with the business. You know how she is."

"Yes, she's too comfortable with the way things are."

"You've got it. She's in her office resting. Go on up, she'll be happy to see you. I'll tell Soledad you're coming."

Adrienne kissed him on both cheeks and threw her arms around his shoulders.

"See you later." She moved across the room to the ornamental doors and opened them.

"Glad to see you home again, Miss Wyngate." Soledad's face lit up with a smile. He was a big man and Adrienne had known him and his family all her life.

She walked silently down the plush carpeted hall and up the stairs, admiring the familiar works of art that adorned the walls of the long corridor. Jolie had a good eye for the finer things in life and had added a few new pieces of art. With the exception of Adrienne's father, her judgment of men was pretty bad. Her thoughts slipped back to the past.

Her father and Jolie had been friends growing up. He was the rich boy, and she was the poor girl. It hadn't mattered to her father. He had liked Jolie for herself.

The senior Wyngate disapproved of Jolie as a wife to the heir of the family dynasty. His heir needed a proper wife to carry on the family name.

Jolie made many mistakes in her young life. After her two failed marriages, she came back to the island and opened the club. Adrienne's father supplied the backing Jolie needed to start her business, and it became a success. She paid him back and became one of the town's successful businesswomen.

Jolie had a way of making friends with everyone. She was known throughout the islands for her hospitality and good food.

People gossiped about her father's friendship with Jolie. The most important person in his life, her mother, understood the bond between them. She never showed any jealousy of the abundantly curvaceous woman.

Her mother also had a friend outside of her marriage to Adrienne's father. Robert Holmes had rescued her mother from being mugged while she attended cooking classes on the main island. Robert and his wife came to visit the island often and decided to stay. They took the old Plantation House and turned it into one of the elite dining establishments on Santa Isabella. Robert and his wife were Adrienne's godparents.

Her father and mother often went away on business trips, and Jolie, her other godmother, would stay with the Wyngate children. After her mother died, Adrienne could confide in Jolie. It made Adrienne respect and love her even more. Jolie never made light of Adrienne's problems and helped her in any way she could. As she grew older, she also understood more about the friendship between her father and this outgoing, vibrant woman.

Adrienne drew in a deep breath before knocking on Jolie's door. The sound echoed in the stillness. With no answer she knocked again, knowing Jolie was probably relaxing or engrossed in one of her novels.

"Whoever you are? Come in before you knock the door down."

Jolie's voice was throatier than Adrienne remembered. She opened the door and entered the room. Jolie, still engrossed in her book didn't bother to look up.

"Is that the way you greet old friends? It must be a great book."

Jolie let out a loud whoop, and her book went skyward. "Adrienne, it's you. You've finally come home." Before Adrienne could move, she was swept into Jolie's ample bosom. "It's good to see you, love."

Her friend squeezed tighter. Adrienne moved out of her embrace and studied her good friend. Jolie wore a long silk caftan in various shades of green that slimmed her ample figure.

Jolie surveyed her young friend, and Adrienne read approval in her eyes.

"You're skinny as a rail." Jolie teased.

"You know it's always been hard for me to gain weight.

"Are you hungry? Do you want to eat? Do you want a drink?" The words tumbled from her mouth.

"Yes, to all of them," Adrienne answered, laughing.

Jolie went over to the intercom and ordered. "Miguel, we need two Tahitian Queens and two lobster salad sandwiches, and hurry. My friend and I are starving." Adrienne smiled at her in agreement.

Jolie looked her up and down. "You look like you have been through a ringer."

It wasn't an insult, just a statement of fact. Adrienne was tired, nervous, and excited. Traveling has a tendency to do that. " I didn't have time to get everything done. I'm going to check into the hotel when I leave here."

"You're staying at the hotel? Does your grandmother know you're here?"

"It's too late to disturb her. I'll see her tomorrow. You know she takes care of business in the morning and doesn't like to be disturbed before ten. I'm sure she already knows I'm here."

"I presume there's a reason you stopped here first instead of heading straight to the hotel?"

"I wanted to see an old friend and…"

"That sounds like a questionable 'and'."

"I met a man on the ferry coming over. He introduced himself as Tyler Prescott. Should I know him? He seemed to know me." She felt embarrassed at bringing up his name.

"Since his arrival on the island, he's become a good friend of your grandmother's."

"Ooh." She didn't want Jolie to know she found Tyler Prescott more interesting then the men she had met lately.

"Aha. He's perked your interest." A smile of mischief appeared on her friend's face.

"No, I'm just curious. You might know who he is." Adrienne tried to appear nonchalant.

"A lot of new people have come to the island to live and work. What's so different about this one?"

"Trinidad met him at the landing. They appeared to know each other quite well."

"Tyler Prescott is more intriguing than any man has a right to be, even with a scarred face. Actually he's quite mysterious." Jolie watched Adrienne's reaction.

"That's the one. He said he owns Hunter's Lodge."

Adrienne was more than inquisitive. He had aroused feelings in her she thought she had lost with Steven's betrayal.

"He was a construction engineer hurt in a bridge accident a few years ago. He's quiet and keeps to himself. He has a partner in Miami who comes and goes. He's an older man with gray hair, quite nice looking in a fatherly way."

"Mr. Prescott sounds interesting."

"He's very rich. All the island mothers with marriageable daughters are inviting him to their social affairs, hoping their little darlings will snag him. He politely refuses, which makes him more intriguing. It's as though he's looking for someone special. You know how it is. There aren't enough eligible bachelors here."

"Even, with his disfigurement?" She saw the way Jolie looked at her.

"Coming from you, that's an unusual comment."

A yawn escaped. "I'm sorry. I'm just overtired."

"Money influences a lot of people," Jolie remarked.

"So they're more interested in his money than him." Adrienne didn't like that.

The food arrived, and they sat down to eat their meal. When they finished, Adrienne was hoping Jolie would drop the matter and talk about something else, but she took up where she left off.

"Tyler arrived on the island about eighteen-months ago and bought Hunter's Lodge.

Tyler had already told her about his home. "The house was a disgrace for years."

"Not anymore. He's remodeled it. I understand he's done a terrific job. He's moved in and plans to stay from what your grandmother told me. The three of them, Charlotte, Alex, and Tyler, are very close."

"That's why Trinidad was at the ferry to meet him."

"They seem to be working on some kind of business deal."

"Alex is always looking for new business," Adrienne said.

"Ever heard of Prescott World Enterprises?"

"No. Should I have?"

"It belongs to Tyler and his partner. They buy up old mansions and renovate them into first-class resorts or expensive homes. The island could use a resort to bring more enterprises. There's no space available."

"The only piece of property big enough to meet his needs is, Wyngate," Adrienne said. "It's not for sale under any circumstances."

"Don't jump to conclusions, my dear. There hasn't been any mention of him wanting to buy Wyngate, but there have been some strange things going on up at the house."

"Oh?"

She wondered if Sir John and the Contessa had been mischievous while she was away. If someone came into the house they didn't like, the house became haunted. She would have to talk to them and find out what was happening.

"There are always rumors. Is that why my grandmother summoned me to come home because of this man, Prescott?"

"I have no idea," Jolie said. "She's never mentioned anything to me. Tyler travels a lot. He seems content when he's here for any length of time."

"Does he live at Hunter's Lodge by himself?"

"No, sometimes his partner comes for a visit, and he's just as private as Tyler. There's a handyman who doesn't look like one. We very seldom see him. It makes us wonder. There are a couple of servants, and they keep to themselves. Tyler has a male nurse named Julio. There are times when Tyler has trouble with his leg and has to use a cane. Julio is a masseur and also acts like a bodyguard. I guess in Tyler's business, he needs one."

"What do you mean?"

"It's like I said, he's rich and buys up the old estates. A time comes when the owners can no longer afford to take care of them, especially if the house has been in the family for generations like Wyngate. For the owners, it's a way of getting fresh money into their hands and getting rid of the monstrosities their ancestors bestowed on them. It causes hard feelings among families when they have to give up their inheritance."

"Wyngate is on solid ground," Adrienne insisted.

"What if something happens to you?"

"It will still be cared for as long as there is a Wyngate. It will stay in the Wyngate family."

"I think you've taken an interest in Tyler." Jolie grinned.

"I have no intentions of getting involved with any man at this time." Drat, she was fibbing. She wanted to know all about Tyler Prescott.

"Your heart doesn't always do what you want," Jolie said with a knowing look.

"I've had a lot of time to think about what happened on my wedding day. I've learned it's better to let go than hold onto things you cannot change."

"Isn't that the truth? Go on up to the hotel. You look beat. I'll have Julio take you."

"No. I'll get a taxi in the square. Thanks for the information." They hugged and kissed goodbye for now.

As Adrienne turned to go, Jolie called out to her. "Be careful." Her voice held more than a note of concern.

"Is that a warning?"

"Take it any way you like, just be careful."

It was early morning when she returned downstairs. The club was closing. Norman let her out with a cherry good night.

Chapter Eleven

The Valencia Hotel, an elegant old lady from the past, stood majestically on a hill above the city. She flaunted her white gingerbread porches for all to see. Surrounded by tall trees, the hotel reminded Adrienne of a large pearl displayed in a bed of lush green velvet. It had been built by one of Adrienne's great-grandfathers more than a hundred years ago. It had two floors and a wide veranda overlooking the antiquated city and harbor of Belle Town.

Several cottages lay scattered among the lush tropical foliage that surrounded the main building. It provided privacy for those who wanted it. Over the years, governors, presidents, and movie stars had sought refuge here. The Valencia, a dignified dowager, loved the attention she received.

Standing in the middle of the sedate lobby, Adrienne surveyed familiar surroundings. An assortment of oriental rugs lay snug on highly polished teak floors. A party of revelers entered the lobby from one of the ballrooms. In the middle of the crowd, she saw a familiar face. James Farnsworth, the hotel manager, walked in her direction. Tall and distinguished with his mop of thick white hair, he stopped in disbelief when he saw her.

"Good grief, Adrienne, is that you? Are my old eyes deceiving me?"

"The one and only." She smiled at him.

"For a moment, I thought I was seeing things." The older man grinned in delight.

"I've come home."

"I'm glad. I hardly recognized you. You're thinner and strikingly beautiful." He reached out to pull her into his arms.

She stepped back. "I'm a little messy. I don't want your suit to get dirty." She let him hold her at arms length.

"You look marvelous. Does your grandmother know you're home?"

"She knows I'm coming. I couldn't give her an exact time for my arrival. She'll definitely know I'm home when we meet later this morning."

"She'll be glad to see you." Happiness showed on his face.

"How is she?" She was anxious to know about her grandmother's health.

"We're getting older and fragile. That left hip gives her some trouble. If she'd use her cane, she wouldn't have so many problems. You know how vain she can be at times. She doesn't want anyone to think she needs to use one."

"Have you ever known my grandmother to obey orders, doctors or otherwise?"

"She never has, my dear. I'm so glad you decided to come home." He hugged her.

"Thank you." It felt good to be back. Did her meeting with Tyler Prescott have anything to do with it?

"Is the Queen's cottage available?"

"Of course, I'll have Ramon take your bags over. They arrived earlier."

"Good." The island's heat and humidity sapped her strength. What she needed was a good hot shower and a change to soft pajamas, a robe, and time to relax.

"Charlotte will be pleased to see you." He kept the conversation going as he escorted her to the cottage.

The scent of flowers and the sea perfumed the night air. The moon and stars shone high above, radiating a silver path of light. Contentment settled over her.

"By now, I'm sure the whole island knows." Adrienne knew how fast news traveled.

"With the island grapevine, I'm sure they do," Mr. Farnsworth agreed. "Old habits die hard. Have you come home for good?" His fatherly concern showed.

"Yes," she assured him.

"We've all missed you. Many things have changed since you went away. This is where you belong, here in Santa Isabella. I am glad you decided to return." He looked at her with troubled eyes. Something worried him.

"Thank you." She'd known him all her life. He was a good friend, yet she sensed uneasiness in him.

"I'll send Camie, Carmen that is, over. She'll help you get settled. Just tell her what you need, and she'll do it." Before she could tell him, she didn't need a maid, his phone beeped.

"Excuse me, my dear." He moved aside and answered his phone. He turned to her. "I have an emergency in the Flamenco Room." He left her at the cottage door.

The spacious cottage had a huge master suite, a dining room, kitchen, a lounging area, and a maid's room. Warm beige with accents of jungle green and blue colored the walls. She opened the shuttered screened windows to let the night breeze flow through. Birds calling to their mates and the insistent murmur of insects were part of the nighttime symphony. It would take time to get used to it again. The cottage would be home for now.

Adrienne expected Charlotte would insist she stay at the beach cottage. She had no intention of staying there and upsetting Charlotte's daily routine. Instead, she intended to reopen the big house.

She started unpacking her carry-on. After removing her makeup and taking an invigorating shower, she sprayed on bug repellent and slipped into a comfortable pair of soft blue cotton pajamas and a matching robe. She lay on the chaise lounge in the patio and watched the full moon. Its bright glow bathed everything in its path. Diamond stars studded the sky. She once again felt at peace with her surroundings. Unwanted thoughts ran through her mind, not only of Tyler Prescott but of her friends and their reaction to her unannounced return.

After the wedding fiasco, it had been difficult leaving behind those she loved. Alex had hired detectives and searched for months, but nothing about Steven was ever found. Yet, as she looked back, the time away gave her a new view of life and a chance to start anew.

She had learned a lot while working in the liquor industry. It kept her in touch with the outside world and gave her the distance she needed to sort out her life. She had enjoyed her work, but was exhausted. Now she could rest and consider her future. It was late and time for bed.

In her room, she threw back the covers and lay down. She had been thinking about going home when she received Charlotte's letter telling her it was time to return. She felt there was more to her grandmother's request. Did Tyler Prescott's interest in Wyngate have anything to do with it?

Tyler was another matter, a little older than she liked. She hadn't been able to get him out of her thoughts since they met. Was it a good sign? Was she getting over Steven's desertion? The man seemed to have a nice personality. She wondered what type of person he was before his disfigurement. There was something familiar about him. She couldn't shake the feeling of having met him before.

Chapter Twelve

The smell of fresh coffee awakened Adrienne. She rose and slipped into her robe and followed the aroma to the kitchen where Carmen was busy fixing a tray for her. Croissants and the coffee's delicious smell welcomed her.

"Good morning, Carmen."

Carmen, her newly acquired maid was in her early twenties. She had the high cheekbones and the pecan colored skin of a true Santa Bellian.

"Mister Farnsworth said I'm to take care of you while you're here."

"That's very kind of him. I shouldn't be much trouble. I'll be gone a lot."

Carmen took the tray with Adrienne's breakfast out to the patio. "If there is anything else you need, I'll be in the kitchen."

"Thank you. I'll be going out after I shower and change. My other suitcases should have been brought up from the hotel."

"Yes, Tomas brought them. Is there anything you need right away?"

"The green outfit will probably need a little pressing."

"I'll take care of it." She smiled at Adrienne.

"Thank you."

The girl seemed to be a willing helper. The coffee was strong and black. She added plenty of sugar and cream. The croissants melted in her mouth, and she savored every mouthful. The fresh papaya, mango, and pineapple were heavenly. It had been awhile since she had fruit this fresh. A leisurely breakfast on the patio was just what she needed.

Tyler Prescott and last night's events were just a memory. What kind of game was he playing? Yet, she suspected he wasn't the type to play games. He'd come right out and tell you what he wanted. Did Tyler figure he had a better shot at Wyngate by courting its owner?

The sound of small birds and animals in the bushes broke the morning quiet. She really didn't need a maid. However, the prestige of being a Wyngate and the heiress to a million-dollar business entitled her to certain privileges. It was one of the customs she would have to get used to again. Now that she was home, she'd miss the fun of being a working girl and having no heavy responsibilities.

After enjoying her breakfast and the quiet serenity of the area, she went inside to shower. She dressed in a matching pantsuit with a printed blouse, sandals, and a bag. The few clothes she had with her would be unpacked, cleaned, and pressed by the time she returned. She needed to shop for a new wardrobe. The clothes she left behind on the island were donated to charity, all except her wedding gown.

The keys to the car she ordered sat on the coffee table. She picked them up as Carmen entered the room.

"Don't worry about keeping the cottage clean. I won't need you all the time. I'm sure Mr. Farnsworth will have more important things for you to do."

"You don't want me?" The girl appeared upset.

"It isn't that I don't want you. There isn't enough work for you."

"I need the job." Tears welled in her eyes.

Her words surprised Adrienne. This was a plea for help.

"Why do you need this job?"

"I don't want Mr. Farnsworth to think I'm incompetent. My mother is sick. I take care of my brother and sister, and I'm their only means of support. Because I work here, they can attend school." She wiped her face with the back of her hand.

Carmen looked to be honest and a hard worker. Adrienne's heart told her not to let the girl go. Once she was settled, she would find a more permanent job for her.

"You can stay."

"Thank you, Miss Wyngate. You won't be disappointed."

"I'm sure I won't." Adrienne gave her a smile of encouragement.

A knock on the door interrupted them. A messenger stood with two florist boxes in his hands. "Flowers for Miss Wyngate." He handed her the boxes.

Adrienne untied the bow and opened the first box to find a Cattleya Orchid sitting among the green grass. She admired the flower and heard Carmen's squeals of joy.

"Such a pretty orchid," she exclaimed. "Someone thinks very highly of you."

Reading the card Adrienne wasn't surprised to see it came from Tyler Prescott. "I just met the man last night."

"He is making a good impression." Carmen handed Adrienne the other box.

This box contained a dozen pink roses and was from her second cousin, Peter. He was her old beau and friend. The word of her return had been telegraphed around the island.

"The roses are pretty."

Yes." Adrienne agreed with Carmen.

Chapter Thirteen

A little later, Adrienne left the cottage and strolled through the gardens toward the parking area. She looked around. Everything appeared calm and serene. Before she reached her car, Adrienne heard Peter's familiar voice.

"What are you doing in town so early?"

She was surprised to see him.

"I heard you'd come home. I wanted to see you. I've missed you so much." He took her in his arms and hugged her. He let her go and looked her up and down. "You're more beautiful than ever."

"Thank you, Peter, for the roses, too." She looked at her old friend who now had prominent crow's feet and lines on his face that hadn't been there before. He looked jubilant and happy. It was then she noticed the other man standing by Peter's car.

Peter saw her quizzical look. "I want you to meet a friend of mine, Alberto Romano. He lives on Martinique and is here on business."

Alberto put his hand out to take hers. She didn't like the feel of it or the look in his eyes. He was a predator. What kind of business had Peter gotten himself involved in other then cattle?

"Are you going see your grandmother?"

"No. It's too early. I have a few things to do first."

"I'll call you, and we can go out after you get settled."

"That would be nice."

He kissed her on both cheeks and got into the car with Alberto. She watched them drive away.

The car Adrienne had ordered was a practical four-door sedan. This early in the day the humidity was already affecting her. Once inside the car, she started the motor and turned on the air conditioner. She waited for it to cool the inside air before leaving. She had one stop to make before going to her grandmother's. The native telegraph would spread the word of what she was doing to anyone who was interested.

Her grandmother would expect the delay. She accepted everything else in life quietly and without fuss.

The road with the overhanging eucalyptus trees provided shelter from the hot sun. It had rained during the night. The freshness of new mown hay filled the air. Descending steadily down into the valley, she stopped at an overlook and gazed at the lush green fields below. She remembered how cool the meadows were in the early morning. In the distance, farms and ranches made a patchwork quilt. She feasted her eyes on familiar landmarks. She couldn't linger too long and made one last sweep of the area before returning to her car.

The Episcopal Church and cemetery lay nestled among a stand of eucalyptus trees. The church was old and made of island wood and stone. Like Wyngate, it had stood for centuries. The church survived on donations from the wealthy families on the island. As far as the Wyngates were concerned, the little church would last forever. There was a new Episcopal church in town for the tourists. Many of the seasoned visitors opted to attend services here with the locals.

The bells in the tower tolled the eight o'clock hour, echoing through the valley. It was an old familiar sound. The mistress of Wyngate had come home. Adrienne parked her car and walked the short distance to the family cemetery. Row on row of Wyngate tombstones stood like soldiers at attention among the soft green grass and flowers that decorated their graves. She looked at the stones dating back to the early eighteen hundreds for Sir John, the gentleman pirate, and his wife, the Contessa Theodora, the founders of Wyngate. The silence soothed her spirits. The birds and the animals were quiet.

Most of her family was buried here with the exception of her brother Elliot whose body had never been found, her Uncle Eric, and her stepmother Francine. She knelt beside the graves and said a prayer.

A man's shadow and a familiar voice greeted her as she rose. "So the message is true."

"Have you ever known it to be wrong, Padre?" Adrienne returned

Father Benson's smile.

"No. After these many years, I should know better." He chuckled.

"Yes. I've returned."

Father Benson had aged since she left. The padre's hair was gray now, and he had a few more wrinkles on his smiling face. He wore a sweatshirt over shorts. He had married her sister to Alex and would have married her to Steven.

"I'm glad you've come home. Your grandmother has missed you."

"Thank you. It's good to be home." She had to keep telling herself this, or otherwise she might run away again. Deep in her heart, she knew she couldn't shirk her duties any longer.

"It was a difficult time for you."

"You needn't worry. I've had plenty of time to bury the past. Going away helped ease the pain." Yet her heart still ached for Steven.

"Is something wrong?"

"No, I've learned to deal with my problems. At one time, I didn't think it would be possible. Like you, I have learned to deal with life and death."

"It's not an easy thing to do," he replied.

"One does many things when it's necessary for survival. The world is a harsh place."

"It looks like you managed fairly well."

"I haven't forgotten what happened, but I've learned to live with it. Brooding over something that wasn't meant to be doesn't help one to move forward."

"You were always a smart young woman." He smiled and offered a benediction.

"I hope I can live up to your belief in me. Goodbye, Padre." She started towards her car and almost didn't hear the Padre's barely audible words.

"Be careful, Adrienne." His voice expressed deep concern and it bothered her.

Back in the car, she turned off the valley road and headed toward her grandmother's. It was going to be a beautiful day, and her thoughts wandered. She enjoyed the scenery as she passed familiar places. There was little traffic as she mulled over the padre's words.

Why would he warn her to be careful? She had just arrived last night and hadn't told anyone that she knew what was coming, yet everyone seemed to know. The island telegraph must be working overtime.

Preoccupied with her thoughts, she didn't notice the old truck trying to overtake her. Suddenly, the truck was close behind her car, pushing her forward.

Why was that damn fool speeding on this part of the highway? The narrow road ran through steep hills with sharp curves. In some places, the ditches were deep and deadly. She shouted at the other driver as the truck moved alongside to pass her. Before she could move out of his way, the driver of the truck deliberately sideswiped her car. She stepped on the brakes as the car went off the road. It spun around and landed in a ditch. Fortunately, this particular ditch wasn't deep. With shaking hands, she turned off the engine and sat still, attempting to calm herself.

A short time later, a car approached and stopped alongside her. A familiar figure got out and approached her. She was glad to see Tyler Prescott.

"What happened? Are you all right?" He leaned in the open window. "Do you want me to call for help?"

"No. Someone deliberately ran me off the road. I'm a little shaken up." Tyler's presence helped calm her.

"Are you sure you're alright?"

She got out of the car and stood on wobbly legs. Tyler took hold of her arms.

"I'm fine," she managed to say.

"Let me see if I can start your car."

Adrienne watched as he tried several times to get it started, but the engine groaned, sputtered, and died. He got out his cell phone and dialed a number. After a hurried conversation, he disconnected.

"It'll take the tow truck about an hour to get here. Where are you headed? I'll give you a lift." He motioned her toward his car.

"I'm going to my grandmother's."

She got in his car and they drove off. She looked at him with a twinkle in her eyes. "What are you doing out here so early this morning?" She hadn't wanted to ask, but her curiosity got the better of her.

"Inquisitive, aren't we?" He was grinning.

"If it was with some mysterious woman, forget I asked." The nervousness was leaving her.

"Would it matter to you?"

With a smile on her face, she avoided the question by not answering.

"I was hoping it would. I was on my way back from looking at a ranch in which I have an interest."

"You don't look like the rancher type." Another smile lifted the corners of her mouth.

"When you get to know me better, you'll find out I'm a lot of things."

"What makes you think I want to know you better?"

"There's a spark between us. You know it as well as I, and I intend igniting the spark and see it burst into beautiful flames." He reached over and caressed her cheek.

She pulled away, not wanting him to know what his touch aroused in her, knowing she already liked the feel of it. "There's nothing between us."

He was getting under her skin, just like Steven did. She didn't want to think of Steven. Damn it.

"Getting to know you is something I intend to remedy as quickly as possible."

"It's one way of getting my attention."

"I would like to take you to dinner some evening."

"You're rushing things." It was the second invitation she had within a few hours.

"With a pretty girl like you, I have to move fast to beat the competition."

"What competition?"

She knew invitations would come pouring in from all the right people, mostly people in whom she had no interest. For some reason, she was hoping he would be the only one to call.

"Adrienne, don't underestimate yourself. You're a beautiful and desirable woman." Tyler paused. "Do my disfigurements bother you?"

"No, on the contrary. I find you intriguing."

"It bothers a lot of people."

"I'm not a lot people." She smiled at him.

Her emotions were surfacing and she couldn't let him see them, not yet. It was much too soon.

"I'm going to be late for an appointment."

"Your grandmother has waited this long. I'm sure she won't mind waiting a few minutes more."

"How do you know how my grandmother feels?" She arched one eyebrow, questioning him.

"We've become good friends. She talks about you all the time."

"Does she?"

Her thoughts were more on him than her visit to her grandmother. He seemed so easy going and direct in what he wanted, but she felt he was hiding something. Whatever his secret was, she intended to learn it.

Chapter Fourteen

On her return from her grandmother's, Adrienne considered what her grandmother had said and how she had appeared. Charlotte came from a long line of strong and willful people. Both sides of the Wyngates were tough. Their ancestors included a mixture of French, English, and Spanish, along with scalawag sea captains and unscrupulous land barons with some nobility thrown in.

Charlotte very seldom pussyfooted around a problem, but she had done so this morning. Adrienne wondered if her return home had triggered the uneasiness she saw in her grandmother's eyes. Why should her grandmother be afraid for her? She had returned at Charlotte's request, and the old woman scolded her for her neglect of Wyngate Manor. Adrienne couldn't see that as the reason for Charlotte's uneasiness.

On her return to the cottage, Adrienne found an excited Carmen. At her grandmother's request, the hotel had sent over an assortment of clothing for her to consider. The maid's enjoyment at seeing all the clothes amused her. If Carmen worked well during her stay, Adrienne decided she would find a permanent place for her at Wyngate Manor.

Adrienne chose a coral silk slack outfit with a shell top and fitted jacket. The material was soft against her skin. She was about to leave the cottage when the telephone rang.

"Welcome home, love." It was Robert, her godfather. His vibrant tones carried over the line.

"Robert, how nice it is to hear your voice."

"I hope I'm not catching you at a bad time."

"I was on my way out."

"Cathy and I were hoping you'd stop by and have dinner with us this evening."

"I'd love to. I'm on my way to see Alex. I'll be there around ten." No Islander had dinner before then.

"We'll be expecting you."

She replaced the phone and thought of Robert and his wife Cathy. The society matrons of the island had a fit when her parents chose them and Jolie to be Adrienne's godparents. Mom and Dad stood by their choices. Adrienne couldn't be happier.

She entered the hotel lobby. Night was approaching, and the hotel was coming to life following the afternoon siesta. She heard snatches of conversation and music as the guests prepared for the evening's activities.

Later, driving through town, she edged through the crowded streets at a slower speed. She had time to look around and see familiar places. Portside buildings had been remodeled and painted.

The late ferry sounded its mournful whistle as it left the dock on its way back to the main Island. Steel bands and Calypso music blended with the sounds of the city. Belle Town, the island's largest city, lay at the foot of the Blanket Mountains surrounding this piece of paradise. It had a strong New England influence. Most of the town touted its English, French, and Spanish heritage. It had grown with the times and had class. The city enforced restrictions for building, so there were no tacky storefronts or shanties. The businesses gleamed with a cleanliness not often found in the Caribbean. Native wood and stucco comprised most buildings. Gaily painted shades of pinks, yellows, blue, orange, lavender and green colored the houses with their white gingerbread porches. They stood against the backdrop of the blue gray mountains and their blanket of green forest.

She soon left the town behind. Once on Ocean Drive, the traffic thinned. When she reached the Casino, the sun was sinking below the horizon. The sea lapped against the jetty that protected the land from the tropical storms, which occasionally ravaged the island. The casino sparkled like a brilliant gem against the darkening night. Lamborghinis, Jags, and Mercedes filled the huge parking lot. Bright lights threw shadows on the palatial lawns, while flowers bordered walks that led to the main entrance.

Adrienne left her car with the parking attendant. She made her way up the marble staircase to the center of the casino. The usual welcomes and good evenings came her way. No one stopped her for conversation. Not being recognized gave her a sense of privacy.

It had been a long time since Adrienne had done any gambling. She tried her luck at blackjack. After losing her few chips, she ordered a drink and sat awhile. She enjoyed watching the crowd before she went upstairs and invaded Alex's privacy.

Seeing him again would bring back unwanted memories for both of them. She wasn't sure she could face him with the tragedy that lay between them. She wanted to delay, but a familiar voice greeted her.

"Miss Adrienne. I'm glad you decided to come home."

"Thank you, Trinidad. It's good to be back."

Trinidad could wear any kind of clothing. He looked magnificent, like he just stepped out of a gentleman's fashion magazine. His height, pecan skin, and blue eyes separated him from other natives with their brown eyes.

"He's waiting for you." Trinidad's teeth shone like brilliant white pearls.

She followed him up the winding staircase and down the hall. He spoke to the guards and then entered the foyer to Alex's apartment. Alex came from an old island family of gamblers. They had owned the casino since it first opened more than two hundred years ago. The legacy passed from father to son and remained strong, but now there were no sons to inherit. The love between him and Aimee had been strong. It was supposed to last a lifetime.

Her sister, Aimee, had been fifteen when she first met Alex. It was love at first sight. She set her cap for him, and he didn't have a chance. The ten-year difference in their ages and what people thought didn't bother them. After they were married, Alex was in seventh heaven when he learned Aimee was pregnant. His happiness was shattered when she and the baby were killed by a hit and run driver.

Alex's life became a nightmare. He went through a period of drinking and depression. He disappeared for a few months. When he returned, he devoted himself entirely to his work. This evening, Alex sat at his desk absorbed in reading. He failed to notice her entrance.

"I expect at least a jolly good hello and how are you."

"Adrienne, sweetheart. It's good to have you home." He rose from his chair, came around the desk, and hugged her. She returned his hug.

"How's that?" He grinned at her.

"It'll do." Adrienne noticed the picture of her sister was missing from his desk. Eight years was more than enough time to mourn the one you love. It hadn't been that long since Steven left. Maybe, she should take the hint. She pointed to the empty spot on his desk and gave him a questioning look.

"Aimee and I had the kind of love many people search for over a lifetime, but I can't mourn forever. It was time to put the past behind me."

"Like so many things in life, it's easier said than done."

Alex appeared nervous. She suspected it was because he'd met someone and didn't know how to tell her.

"What's the name of the lady who has captured your heart?"

He didn't look surprised. "Her name is Lindsey Tanner, and she's new to the island. She's just a few years younger and is a widow with two children, a boy and a girl." He grinned.

"That's wonderful, Alex. I wish you happiness. When can I meet her?"

"It will be very soon, and thank you."

"Does the rest of the family know?"

"It's gotten around that we're seeing each other."

"Then I won't have to worry about saying anything out of turn." She smiled at him, glad he had found someone at last. "This morning, Peter hailed me in the parking lot of the hotel."

"Are you going to pick up where you left off with him?"

"There is nothing but friendship between us."

"You may think so, Adrienne, but I don't think Peter believes it."

"I'm sure he's found someone one else by now. Anyway, I'm not ready for dating. There are too many others things that need my attention."

"I heard you met my friend, Tyler Prescott." Alex looked serious.

"Yes, he's making quite an impression. He sent me my favorite orchids."

"You don't sound overly thrilled."

"Should I be? I understand he's interested in Wyngate."

"If he is, he hasn't mentioned it to me."

"How strange? If he's a friend, I think he would have mentioned it."

"I know he's interested in two pieces of property on Santa Maria." He rubbed his chin in thought.

"Perhaps. When anybody hears the name Wyngate, their eyes light up like stars. You can tell him to stop pursuing me. I'm not interested."

"Tyler's pursuing you?" Surprise showed on Alex's face. "In what way?"

"He seems to be every place I am."

"Maybe he likes you."

"More like Wyngate."

"He's not that kind of man."

Adrienne looked at her brother-in-law and smiled. She suspected Alex knew exactly what Tyler was doing.

"You can tell him to quit wasting his time."

"I haven't seen him in days. I presume he had other plans."

"Good. Then we won't have the pleasure of bumping into each other."

"He's a great guy when you get to know him."

"What makes you think I want to know him?" She had a sarcastic lilt to her voice.

It was a relief to know she wouldn't be seeing Tyler Prescott this evening. She had enough trouble keeping him out of her thoughts. He was an imposing man and a little arrogant. He was too sure of himself for her liking, but something about him drew her. Adrienne didn't stay long knowing Alex was busy.

* * * *

Peter greeted her as she entered the main part of the casino. "Adrienne, darling, I didn't expect to see you so soon."

Peter and his friend had just entered the main lobby. As usual, Peter kissed her on both cheeks.

"I was visiting Alex."

"I haven't seen him in ages. He stays locked up in his office most of the time."

"I'm sure he gets out once in awhile."

"Why don't you join us and do a little gambling?" Peter suggested."

"I'm not much for gambling. Good luck."

Before she could leave, Peter grabbed her arm and pulled her close. "When can we get together for dinner?" Peter's friend lingered in the background. "Just you and I, Adrienne."

"That would be nice. Call me, and we'll set up a time."

Chapter Fifteen

On her way through the hills to the Plantation House Restaurant, Adrienne couldn't help but think of Tyler. When the chance came, she would ask him why he wanted Wyngate. It would take the fun out of the game he was playing. No, on second thought she decided she wouldn't do it. Hearsay wasn't proof. She'd have to hear it from his lips, before she would do anything.

He seemed to be straightforward in his advances toward her. Why not play along? She wasn't dumb enough to think he was attracted to her when her money and Wyngate loomed in the background. Yet she didn't want to believe it was his only reason for seeing her. She couldn't let her heart go to a man who was only after her money.

Maybe, Alex was right, and Tyler did like her. Her grandmother said he was wealthy. Maybe he needed more because some business deal had gone wrong. He wouldn't be the first one who wanted Wyngate for the prestige it brought. Weighing the circumstances, she had to give him the benefit of the doubt. Jolie and her grandmother were seldom wrong in their judgment of people.

Eucalyptus trees formed a tunnel shutting out most of the moonlight. She hoped she wouldn't meet anyone who was in a hurry.

The trees opened up, and the moon bathed the Plantation House in a glow of yellow light. Surrounding trees swayed in the evening breeze and traced intricate lacy patterns against the darkness. A wide open space of well manicured lawns surrounded the low flung house. She recognized the dark green foliage of hibiscus, orchids, and bougainvillea. They emitted a heady, enticing fragrance that put her in a romantic mood and wishing she had someone with whom to share the evening.

She followed the lighted curving drive to the parking lot below the terrace. It was difficult finding a place to park. Well-lit stone steps led up to the terrace. Paths branched off in different directions, leading to beautiful flower gardens where water fountains whispered to the night breeze.

The sound of laughter and the murmur of conversation carried over the soft background music. On the terrace, candles surrounded by exotic flowers, glowed and flickered on tables covered in white damask cloths. It was a setting made for romance.

There were many couples holding hands, obviously enjoying each other's company. It made her envious, and she felt out of place.

For a moment she regretted accepting Robert's invitation. She was here now and would have to make the best of it. She thought she could claim fatigue and leave early, but that wouldn't be fair to Robert. He would have a special meal waiting for her.

Victor, the headwaiter, greeted her with joyous enthusiasm. "It's good to have you back, Miss Wyngate. We've missed you."

"Thank you, Victor. It's good to be back."

"Mister Robert is so excited. He's been fussing at Cedric all night."

"Tell Cedric I appreciate all his hard work. I'm sure the meal will be perfect."

"He'll be pleased to hear your compliments. Please, come this way."

She followed Victor to a table at the far side of the terrace. He held a chair out for her while she sat down. A spray of orchids lay by her place with a note, which she read. It's good to have you back. It was signed by the staff.

"How sweet of them to remember me." She smiled up at Victor as he fussed around her.

Robert arrived a few minutes later with her favorite drink, a Caribbean Queen. Placing her drink on the table, he leaned over and kissed her on both cheeks.

"Hello, Robert. Please thank the staff for the lovely orchids."

"You're welcome, my dear."

"Where's Cathy?"

"Robbie's giving her a difficult time. He has a slight cold and is fussing. He's almost five now."

"At that age, they can be a handful. I'll call her, so we can get together soon."

"She'll like that. Darling, you look absolutely fabulous in that coral outfit."

"Thank you."

Their dinner arrived, and she raved about the meal. They talked about trivial and unimportant things.

"We're glad you decided to come home. Your grandmother and your friends have missed you."

"I needed to get away."

"I know. Alex wasn't able to find out what happened to Steven."

"Going away was good for me. I learned there is another world out there. I did some traveling on my own and discovered what I thought I was missing. I had to come home. This is where I belong."

They were having coffee and dessert when a buzz went through the crowd of diners. She looked up to see Tyler escorting a blonde woman. She recognized the blonde as Collette Morrison, a fellow islander Adrienne knew slightly. A flash of jealousy took her by surprise.

Why should she care who Tyler dated? She wanted him to leave her alone. Yet, did she really want him to leave her alone? She had a hard time trying to convince herself.

"Darling, you look miffed. I wouldn't worry about Collette. She's only his secretary."

"What makes you think I'm miffed?"

"It's all over the island that he's pursuing you."

"He's doing it without any luck," she responded.

"I'm not so sure about that."

"I think the night air, the good food, and drinks are getting to me," Adrienne offered as an excuse to leave.

"Most likely your body clock hasn't adjusted to our time. It generally hits the tourists a few days after they arrive."

"I guess that's it. Do you mind if I leave?"

"I understand. Cathy and I will make arrangements to meet you at another time."

"Thanks, Robert." She kissed him on both cheeks and left.

There was no way she could avoid passing Tyler's table. She braced herself. He simply nodded his head in acknowledgment and let her pass. She sighed with relief even though she was disappointed.

Walking down the stairs, she passed a smooching couple. The night had grown darker. The lights along the path had gone out. She had an odd sensation of being watched. Wearing heels, Adrienne was less sure-footed than usual.

She sensed someone on the steps behind her. Without warning, something or someone pushed her forward.

"What the ..." A terrified scream, cut off at intervals as she tumbled down the remaining stone steps.

Crumpled in a heap at the bottom of the stairs, disoriented and in pain, Adrienne realized people were around her who wanted to help. Her mind was fuzzy.

Just before passing out, she imagined she heard Steven whisper "Cara Mia."

Chapter Sixteen

The sun was high in the sky when Adrienne woke. The aches and pains warned her not to move too quickly. What had happened?

Then she remembered falling. She opened one eye and then the other. Why was she at her grandmother's house instead of the hotel? Carmen, with a worried look, sat in a chair across from her.

"Why ... are you here?"

"Thank goodness, you're awake." A big smile replaced Carmen's worried frown. "Your grandmother is resting."

"What time is it?"

Adrienne slowly brought herself up to a sitting position. What caused all the aches and pains? Then she remembered. Did she fall that hard?

"It's twelve-thirty," Carmen answered. "Just in time for lunch."

"What am I doing at my grandmother's?"

Charlotte entered the room. "Don't blame her. She followed Doctor Hall's orders."

"What am I doing here?" Adrienne repeated.

"You were at the Plantation House and fell down those steep stone steps. Tyler brought you here. You were shaken up and conscious when Doctor Hall examined you. He said for you to take it easy for a day or two."

"Tyler brought me here?" Adrienne was astonished. "How the devil did he accomplish it? He was having dinner with Collette."

"That's interesting. He was alone when he brought you here," Charlotte said.

Adrienne was happy at the thought of Tyler leaving Collette to bring her here. Collette must have been fuming.

"How could I have fallen?"

Adrienne remembered leaving shortly after her dinner with Robert. Her mind was on several things. Tyler entertaining Collette had sent a stab of jealousy through her.

Steven had been a handsome man. She had never had this feeling when he was attentive to other women. What was wrong with her?

"I was on my way down the terrace steps to the parking lot when I lurched forward. I must have tripped on something." She could remember feeling the barest touch of a hand between her shoulders before she fell.

"Is something wrong? You suddenly turned pale."

"No. I'm just tired. Too much excitement."

"It's a good reason for letting you sleep late. Robert called to see how you were. He said you looked exhausted at dinner. Cathy sends her love. Peter also called. He heard the news and was worried about you."

"I was more tired than I realized. I'll call Peter later."

"Do you feel up to eating?"

"Oh, yes."

Adrienne didn't tell Charlotte about someone pushing her because it would upset her. Who had spoken those endearing words to her? Tyler was holding her in his arms. Why did he call her, "Cara Mia?" Steven often used those words. Trying to figure it out made her lightheaded.

Her mind wandered. She missed what Charlotte was saying. They were watching her. "Darling, I think you had better take it easy for the rest of the day."

"I'll be fine after a good meal."

"Do as you're told and behave yourself." Charlotte's voice held a warning.

Carmen set the table on the patio. Adrienne made it to the table without any help. She and her grandmother enjoyed the cold lunch Joseph had prepared. It was like old times sitting here, talking, and looking out onto the sandy beach and surf. It was peaceful. Even Wyngate by the Sea looked inviting.

Adrienne's life hadn't been this peaceful for a long time. She made up her mind to find out who was trying to frighten her and why. She grew restless and agitated, but managed to finish her lunch and carry on a conversation with her grandmother.

"If you don't feel up to it, I'll cancel tomorrow night's party," Charlotte said.

"Don't do that. It'll be nice seeing our friends again. It'll give me a chance to catch up on their lives and the local gossip."

She was eager to see her old acquaintances. Yet one of them could be her enemy. In a conversation with her guests, she might learn something that would guide her.

"Can I borrow your keys to the house?"

Charlotte looked startled at Adrienne's request. Her grandmother was about to say something, but seemed to think better of it.

"Now is a good time as any to chase away the ghosts of the past."

"You're not fit to go anywhere."

"I'm fine, just a few nicks and bruises, nothing major. I feel good. See my foot is all right." She wiggled it around for Charlotte to see and tried not to wince.

"Alright, if you must go. Trying to keep you from doing what you set your mind to was always difficult." Charlotte went inside and returned with the keys.

"I saved your wedding gown. It was too lovely to let go. I had it treated and sealed. It's hanging in your cedar closet."

"I'm glad you did. It's a gorgeous gown."

"Are you sure you want to go to up there today? It looks like a storm is brewing."

"There's nothing to fear there. We lived in the house for years."

Carmen came in with a florist box in her hands. "This came for Miss Adrienne." She handed the box to Adrienne.

She didn't sit down to open the gift. There was no card identifying the sender. She thought it was another orchid from Tyler. She untied the ribbon and lifted the cover off the box. She separated the tissue paper and stepped back. A startled scream escaped her throat. The box fell to the floor. A large black-widow spider crawled out of the paper.

The spider didn't have much chance to crawl away before Carmen stepped on it. She looked up into the white face of her employer.

"Madre de Dios! Who would want to send you a deadly spider?"

Adrienne looked at her grandmother and saw fear in her eyes. As a child, Adrienne had developed a fear of spiders crawling over her after she was locked in the cellar years ago.

In the States, she had taken a special course on spiders, so she could understand them and treat their bites with some authority. This spider had surprised her. She still didn't like the creepy things.

"I don't know who delivered it," Carmen said. "When Raymond went to cut flowers for the table he found it by the front door." The girl was upset.

"Thank you. That will be all, Carmen."

Charlotte made sure Carmen had left the room before speaking. "It must have been delivered by hand. Who would do such a ghastly thing?" Her voice faltered.

"Someone isn't happy about my return home," Adrienne said. "I wish I knew why. It might clear up things."

"That's ridiculous. You have no enemies," her grandmother insisted.

"It seems I do." She rubbed her hands together.

"Are you going to call the police?"

"Not yet. If something more serious happens, I'll be forced to notify the authorities."

Charlotte paled.

"I better call Peter and let him know I'm all right."

She went to the phone and dialed the number her grandmother handed her.

"Peter, how are you? I'm fine, just a little shaken up. Dinner tomorrow night will be great. See you then."

Shortly afterwards, Adrienne left her grandmother's and walked along the shore towards Wyngate. Her thoughts were in turmoil. First, the car accident, then the fall down the steps at Robert's, and now the spider. Who hated her so much they wanted to harm her? With some reluctance, she considered her friends and relatives.

Simone, her childhood friend, had been engaged to her brother, Elliot. After his death, Simone married Gene Sinclair. When he died, she inherited his ranch, which was right next to hers. Her land increased by several thousand acres.

George, a distant relative, was an interior decorator. He was ambitious and doing well. He was known to escort some of the prettiest and richest ladies on the island. Yet none of them captured his heart. He seemed comfortable being single.

Everyone once thought Peter Llewellyn and Adrienne would marry. Peter owned a large cattle ranch in the valley, but was often away on business. She had refused his offer of marriage several times, and they remained friends. He had inherited money and appeared content with his life. She ignored the rumors about Peter's unsavory friends. However, meeting his friend the other day made her wonder. What would have been the outcome if she had married Peter? For the present, she hadn't been able to refuse his offer of dinner.

Adrienne knew some women preferred to stay single. For her to have a legal heir, marriage was necessary. In her heart, she wanted a husband and children. She was twenty-six and still had time to find the right man. Maybe she already had. Tyler appeared to be an eligible candidate despite her instincts telling her he only wanted Wyngate Manor.

She had the feeling he was playacting for her, but why? She couldn't think of any reason why he would.

She surveyed the world around her and the prospects for Wyngate Manor. The house knew she had come home to stay. It's strange how through the years the love for things could change. She looked at the mansion in a different light. She still loved its beauty and elegance, but not quite as much as she once had.

It was old and dependent, like an aging parent. It was an expensive burden to support. Was this the way middle-aged children looked at their parents? They wait and hope to find a solution to their problems. Deep in her heart, she couldn't let the house go. Adrienne would keep the old lady until she no longer had any options. Damn it, but she did.

If necessary, she'd take the steps so the mansion would no longer be a burden to future generations. She'll either sell it or give it to the Historical Society. For now, she had plans to make.

Chapter Seventeen

Walking along the beach, Adrienne slipped her sandals off and slung them over her shoulder. The tranquil aquamarine sea lured her into the surf. Bubbles washed against her ankles. Their coolness refreshed against the heat.

Nearing Wyngate, she left the water and climbed the rocky path up the side of the cliffs. Wild birds sang to each other. The cool lush greens of the forest wrapped around her as she slowly made her way. She stopped long enough to catch her breath and inhale the heady fragrances of the flowers that flavored the air. It brought back pleasant memories.

Birds fluttered between the leafy plants and their songs melded with the breakers below. The climb was steep, and she was out of breath when she reached the top.

Closing her eyes to stop the dizziness, Adrienne paused. When she opened them, there sat her ancestral home, Wyngate Manor. She reveled in the beautiful sight. The big stone and wood house stood resplendent in her setting, flaunting her aged beauty over everything around her.

Adrienne inspected the house with its weather-beaten shutters and old stone. Weeds overcrowded the gardens. The remaining flowers grew wild against the galleria. The ruins of stone statues and dried up pools shimmered before her in the hot sun. Only the sound of the breaking waves crashing against the jagged rocks below broke the stillness and smoothed the rock's rough edges.

Dusting off debris from a step, she sat down on the hot marble and surveyed the scene around her. The house was old and neglected, like a debutante past her prime, sad and lonely. She wondered if her forbearers condemned her for deserting her ancestral home.

The sun played tricks with her eyes. It was all there before her. The happy days of her childhood called out to her. She heard her family clearly, ever so clearly.

* * * *

Her brother, Elliot called to Aimee. "Come and see the lizard. Don't bring Adrienne. She's afraid of crawly things."

"Take us out to the Virginia Lady. We can dive off her, please, Daddy. We want to go."

"I'll take you all out, even Adrienne and Simone." He shared his smile of happiness with all of them.

"Why do the little kids have to come along? It should be only for the big kids."

"Elliott, don't talk about the girls that way. When you grow up, my son, you'll learn to appreciate pretty girls."

"They're a pain in the neck," Peter said.

"I assure you, in a few years, you'll change your minds."

* * * *

"Let's play croquet with grandpa. He always lets us win. Doesn't he, grandma?"

"I want the red ball." Simone pouted.

"No. You always want the red ball. Give somebody else a chance."

"Oh, let her have it, Elliott, or she'll pout all day," Peter said.

"Adrienne, behave yourself or Mom won't let us have the party," Aimee scolded.

"Yes, she will. It's my birthday," Adrienne replied.

Her father smiled down at her. "What a beautiful dress my little girl is wearing."

"I love you, Daddy." Adrienne hugged her father.

"And I love you. Here comes your mother. Doesn't she look pretty too?"

Looking at her mother triggered more memories

"I know it's cloudy out, and you don't want to go out and play. At least be a little quieter. Your father is trying to work."

"Yes, Mother," the children answered in unison.

"Go play in the music room. There's plenty of space, and it's sound proof. That way you won't bother your father."

"Come on, Adrienne, let's go to the cellars. We can play hide and seek. There are a lot of neat places to hide," Peter said.

The laughter and love resounded through her head. Oh, what happy days they had been. Where had it all gone? Ghosts of the past called to her to remember. So many happy times and then times changed. They became memories.

The house had many secret passages, large closets, and the storerooms in the cellars. Peter, Adrienne, her brother, and sister played hide-and-seek in the caves.

Adrienne followed Peter to the caves below the house. Peter ran off and left her alone. She ventured into one of the rooms. The door slammed behind her. She tried opening the door, but it wouldn't budge. She banged on the door and screamed.

No one answered her.

She tried not to think about spiders and crawly things. She hated them. An hour or two later they found her. The incident changed her.

To prevent it happening again, her father sealed the passages and locked storerooms. Was it possible someone had found a way through one of the passages into the house?

The stories of the 'Dead Man's Gold' were just that. Her father had researchers review the family archives. They found nothing of a hidden treasure. Over time, many people still tried to gain entrance to the estate looking for it.

* * * *

Adrienne wondered if Simone ever reminded Peter about the nasty things he used to say to her. Strange how life never turned out the way one thought it should.

She remembered her mother and father and the love they shared. She remembered them being scolded by her grandparents for spoiling the children. They were raised with a loving strictness that stayed with them all through their lives.

Then, Momma fell down the stairs and broke her neck. Daddy was inconsolable. Sadness came to dwell at Wyngate Manor.

Daddy's second cousin, Yvette tried to console him. There was just friendship between them. Yvette was in love with someone else. Daddy finally pulled himself together and went on a business trip to Paris. When he came home, he brought Francine, his new French bride to Wyngate.

At first, Adrienne and her siblings were upset, but soon learned to accept their new stepmother. Daddy hoped his bride would bring new life to Wyngate. She did for a while. The house took on a whole new look. Her father hadn't been this happy in a long time. It was good to see him like his old self again. Everyone was happy for him.

Francine and Daddy loved to entertain and have parties. Again, Wyngate sparkled at being the social center of the island.

It was Daddy's birthday. The family celebrated with a big party in the gardens. As the largest plantation owner on the island, Daddy often held a fiesta or a costume ball where everyone was invited to join in the merriment. There was plenty of food and drink. It lasted all day and night and into the next morning. The servants mingled with the elite. Some of the costumes were extravagant, and there were many clowns, pirates, and beautiful women dressed as sirens or queens, and everyone danced to the calypso and steel bands. The crowd had been loud and boisterous.

On the night of the party, Francine danced with Daddy. They were happy. They changed partners. That was the last time anyone saw her.

A note found by one of the servants indicated Francine was unhappy and she was returning to France. She hoped Daddy would understand and wouldn't follow her.

The police investigated and found no clues to her disappearance. A woman of her description was seen boarding the ferry to the big island. As far as the police were concerned, there was no foul play. She left the island of her own free will.

The thing that bothered Daddy the most was that Francine had given him no indication she was unhappy. She left behind all her jewelry. The only things missing were her purse, several thousand dollars, and a small overnight bag. The family was devastated.

The detectives Daddy hired found no trace of her. He was heartbroken. He struggled to keep from letting his grief overcome him.

Losing Francine and then Aimee shortly after in a terrible accident kept the family in mourning.

A few years later, Elliott's tragic accident brought Daddy's lingering illness to an end. Then, grandfather's heart attack killed him. So much tragedy in so short time was too much for the family to bear.

Adrienne and her grandmother had survived. They closed Wyngate by the Sea and moved into the beach cottage. None of the puzzles of long ago had ever been solved. Now, a new one confronted her. Who was Tyler Prescott? What was he really after? Did he want Wyngate to tear it down and build a fashionable resort or was there some other reason? She was sure he was hiding something, but she didn't know what.

The thought of selling Wyngate never entered her mind until she was talking with her grandmother. For her grandfather, the house had never been a burden. When grandfather died, it was left to the oldest son, her father. Adrienne often saw her father looking out to sea, with a wistful look. Wondering what it would have been like to do what he wanted. Uncle Eric had captured his dream of going to sea under dire circumstances. Had he really died at sea as the authorities claimed?

Selling her home would be something she'd have to think about before making any decisions. The sun hid behind threatening clouds. The sea far below called to her. The breakers smashed savagely against the algae-covered rocks, and the churning tide pulled them back only to converge on the rocks again.

The wind whipped her hair against her face. She sat there waiting for the storm's fury to intensify just as it had that night long ago. It would blow over as fast as it started.

The island had changed. It knew she had come home to stay. An odd feeling of unease came over her. Her coming home had lit a fuse somewhere. She would have to wait for it to ignite and burn. She had a feeling she wouldn't have long to wait.

She had loved this island. She no longer loved it the same as she once had. At one time, the island and its people had been her life. She was a woman who no longer looked at it through the colored glasses that she had worn all her young life.

Wyngate Manor

She walked back down the cluttered stone path to the beach below and gazed about her. Gray clouds hugged the sky. The sun was slowly reaching for the sea. Carrying her sandals, she walked into the warm water. The waves licked around her feet, begging her to come and play in their waiting arms. Stepping out of the water onto the wet packed sand, she turned and looked up at the house. In the twilight, the sun reflected on the window where its shutters had broken off. Grotesque shadows danced across the windows, and she glimpsed someone at the window calling to her.

"Adrienne, wait. Please come back. Don't leave me, again."

Chapter Eighteen

Tyler watched the sea caress the shore of the tiny Caribbean island of Santa Isabel. Darkness quickly covered the coastline as the night took on shape and substance. Lights twinkled from boats anchored out in the bay. They joined the lights along the coast to form a necklace of sparkling jewels against the darkened night. It was easy to see why one would fall in love with this piece of heaven.

Voices, mingling with laughter and music, floated across the inlet along with the cool tropic breezes. Tyler didn't notice the laughter and the music coming from the yachts anchored in the distance. For in this partially silent world, his thoughts were elsewhere.

At the age of thirty-eight, his muscular build overcame his deformities. His copper-colored skin came from long exposure to the sun. Some likened him to a fearless pirate who had seen too many battles and knew the price of life. Many of his adversaries learned to beware his face. He observed everything about a person without them knowing it.

The palm fronds whispered back and forth in the night like the touch of a woman's sensuous body. He thought of Adrienne. She was the only woman who could fill the emptiness in his heart. He had everything any man could want, education, money, and position, but, not the woman he loved.

When she learned the truth, would she turn to him with love or hate? He hoped the first. He loved her with all his heart and soul. He planned to woo her and win her love. He was more than ready to settle down and start a family. He knew she wanted a family and an heir. She was the key to the puzzle he'd been trying to solve for the last three years.

Uncle Charlie had hired the best detectives in the business. The culprits' who killed Steven had already been murdered execution style. The person who had hired them probably had them killed.

It had been a long wait for Adrienne to return to her enchanted island. She was leery of him and thought he was only interested in Wyngate and the rumors of buried treasure. He was, but not for the reasons she believed. How would she react when she learned he planned to marry her? He was not interested in Sir John's 'so-called' hoard of gold. He had enough money to support Adrienne and a family.

Her return had put her in danger. Her fall at the Plantation House and the spider incident worried him. Charlotte had good reason to tell him about the unwanted gift. He would take every precaution to protect Adrienne.

Earlier this year, when Tyler was in Norfolk, Virginia, scouting out a project, information reached him about Adrienne. She was working at Ballads, an importer of fine liquors. It was the type of work she liked. She was happy and enjoyed her job. He hadn't tried to contact her. She hadn't overcome her distrust of men.

Would he ever feel the touch of her soft lips on his as he dreamed of so many times? He knew he couldn't go on wanting her without having her. He hoped he wouldn't have a long wait. He had the picture she sent to Steven sitting on his desk at Hunter's Lodge. It was a picture of a young woman in love. How could a woman in her position accept him as he was? Yet, it didn't appear to bother her.

A soft sigh escaped him. He didn't mind the long walk down the white sandy beach to Charlotte's cottage sitting at the far end of the Wyngate Estate. He was taking a chance doing it. He hoped his leg wouldn't give out. The cane helped.

The limp was another reminder of how fragile life could be. Taking the beach route also gave him a chance to pass Wyngate standing alone on the cliffs above like a fortress against the night. He needed entrance to the house to discover what it was hiding. He believed it held the answers to some of the tragedies that plagued Adrienne's family. Was he wrong in his assumptions? He had to be certain.

Adrienne disappeared after she left the island. All letters from her came through a lawyer in Miami with no return address. She didn't want anyone to know where she was. She also didn't want anything happening to Charlotte. Her grandmother was the only person she had left to love.

With his scarred face and limp, what kind of a chance would he have with a beautiful woman like Adrienne? She was compassionate and understanding. She said his infirmities didn't bother her. Most women shied away from anything imperfect. He was far from perfect, but he would stop at nothing to win her love.

It had taken a lot of manipulating and promises to people in high places to locate her. With the help of Alex, it wasn't hard for Charlotte to convince Adrienne to come home. Tyler wanted to prove there was a plan put into motion years ago by an obsessive maniac.

Adrienne's independence and her knowledge of business would take some convincing to get her to agree with his idea. Her life depended on it, whether she liked it or not.

In her absence, the house had been securely locked with an alarm system and checked regularly by a security team. Still, it hadn't prevented someone from entering. On different nights and times, people had seen lights in the old house. The lights were mostly in Adrienne's bedroom. Someone had a key or a way of entering. These questions were upper most in his mind. Tyler looked at the glowing hands on his watch and realized he had dallied too long and must hurry.

Charlotte protected her granddaughter with the fierceness of a mother tiger. Throughout her young life Adrienne managed to survive the heartaches life had imposed on her. No attempts on her life were made while she was in the States. Her problems started again when she came home.

A plan had been set in motion. The woman he loved was in danger.

The sound of voices, mingled with laughter and music grew louder. He walked along the terrace into a room of happy people who pretended friendship. Which one of them was Adrienne's enemy? Who wanted Wyngate so much they would kill for it?

Chapter Nineteen

Entering the room at the beach cottage, Tyler found it crowded with old friends of Adrienne's and her grandmother.

"Tyler, it's nice to see you, again. We're glad you're back," someone said.

"We were beginning to wonder if you'd make it," came from another

"Charlotte, I'm sorry I'm late. It's such a lovely evening. I decided to walk along the beach."

"You didn't miss anything." Her lovely smile assured him. "You have only missed the local gossip."

He liked Charlotte Wyngate. She never seemed to get flustered. If you spilled wine on her best Madeira tablecloth or arrived late like he had tonight, she never scolded. Tall and regal, she walked with the smooth ease of a sleek racehorse, head held high. Her cane was not in view tonight. In her smiling suntanned face, laugh lines edged her deep blue eyes.

For a woman of such wealth, he'd would expect a reserve and haughtiness towards less fortunate people. Charlotte was her natural self. She enjoyed life to its fullest. She had been athletic in her younger days. She still liked to swim and keep fit. She wouldn't let age stop her. Charlotte was born with money, and marrying money hadn't kept her isolated from the world around her. Many of the Wyngate millions were set aside for the island's charitable organizations. For all her gentleness, she was known to have a stubborn streak and a fair mind when dealing in business.

The mayor of Belle Towne, John Thomas, and his wife Darla joined them. The mayor's smile reflected fellowship with those around him. He was an honest man who had done a lot for Belle Towne. He welcomed Tyler.

"My friend, are you going to stay awhile?"

"I'm seriously thinking about it. It's time for a vacation." Tyler's smile embraced those around him. He had more invitations then he could handle from desperate mothers with marriage in mind.

"You're taking a vacation? A workaholic like you never takes time off. Something must have brought you back," the mayor's wife said with a smile.

"The island's beauty is a tonic for me. I miss it when I'm away."

"You've got more blarney than an Irishman," Jolie said, as she joined the group.

Everybody knew Jolie enjoyed her chef's cooking for she was robust in every sense of the word. She had a great personality and was one of the Island's best hostesses.

"Sorry about that, I'm a Scotsman."

"So you're staying this time?" Jolie's smile was mischievous.

"I'll be home for a while," he replied.

"Good, there must be a reason behind this sudden return."

"What makes you think there's a reason?"

"I'd say the young lady across the room would be a very good reason."

"Do you think I'm interested in Adrienne?"

"Yes, I think you're quite smitten with her. You're just what she needs."

"I hope so. Can I trust you to keep your suspicions to yourself?" He winked at her.

"There's more to this than meets the eye. I'll keep my silence, but I promise you one thing. If you ever hurt her, I'll take measures to make sure you never do it again."

Those were strong words for Jolie. Tyler knew she meant everything she said. She loved Adrienne as if she were her own child.

"I promise." He had no sooner gotten the words out than Adrienne approached.

"Is this a private conversation or can anyone join in?"

Adrienne's smile sent Tyler's heart pounding. Damn, he wished this didn't happen every time she came near him.

"Tyler was just telling me about his latest adventure. He makes me wish I were twenty years younger.

"What adventure would that be?" Adrienne used her midnight blue eyes to her best advantage.

"I'm going to stay on the island for a while to decide what I would like to do for my next project. My partner wants to invest in more property here. There is little land available that would meet our needs."

"What are you looking for?" The steeliness in Adrienne's voice was noticeable. Even Jolie looked at her in amazement.

"Adrienne, mind your manners." Jolie admonished. "Please, excuse me. I must talk to Charlotte."

Tyler was trying not to react to Adrienne's nearness. He challenged her. "You don't like me very much, do you?"

Adrienne's eyes widened, but she kept her smile in place.

"It's difficult to judge someone you barely know."

"Have you already made up your mind?"

No, I've just met you. I try not to make hasty judgments until I know a person better. I'm often sorry when I make snap judgments. I think you're hiding something, and you prefer people not to know what's behind that handsome face."

"You think I'm handsome?" This surprised him. No one had told him he was handsome in years. Most people who didn't know him shied away.

"You're definitely handsome. Excuse me. I see someone I must speak to."

"I'll join you."

Before she could refuse, he took her arm. They walked across the room to greet Robert and Cathy.

Cathy hugged and kissed her. "Darling, you look fabulous in blue."

"Thank you. I'm glad you like it." Adrienne looked pleased. "Have you met my friend, Tyler Prescott?"

"Yes, we know Tyler quite well. He's made a good name for himself on the island. It's good to see you back home."

"Nice seeing you again, Robert," Tyler remarked in a friendly manner.

"How's the little guy?" Adrienne said.

"He's much better. One day he's up and the next down with the sniffles."

"You're looking much better than the last time I saw you," Robert observed.

"I'm fine, just too much excitement. I've had a good rest and feel great."

The Reverend Benson greeted her with affection. "It's nice to see you again. You're looking chipper and rested, I must say. Tyler, it's good to see you."

"Thank you," they said in unison.

The padre shook hands with Adrienne.

She turned to his wife, Louisa. "I've heard you have another child."

"A son, he's absolutely beautiful."

"I'm so happy for both of you."

George Farnsworth, Charlotte's constant companion, greeted them. He hugged Adrienne close and smiled at Tyler. They talked a few minutes, before they were greeted by other guests.

Simone hadn't arrived yet, neither had Peter nor Alex. Alex's business always made him late for social affairs. He ran his operation with the skill of a master craftsman and always accepted Charlotte's invitations. He would be arriving soon, Tyler thought to himself as he surveyed the room.

People mingled and picked up conversations where others left off. The food and drinks flowed freely. The evening rushed forward, fueled by food and laughter. Some of the most elite people on the island were in attendance.

Simone, Adrienne's vivacious friend, entered the room exuding a charge of excitement among the guests. Tyler watched as Simone made her way toward them with Peter in tow. He was surprised to see them together because they had never liked each other. Simone always liked men and basked in their admiration of her beauty. Her manner was friendly and exciting.

"Adrienne, darling, I'm so happy." Before Adrienne could reply, Simone continued. "It's been absolutely dull and lonely without you."

They hugged and kissed. Adrienne pulled away from her friend. Peter gave her a big hug and kiss, then let her go."

"Hello Tyler. I see you've found your way back to our lovely island."

Tyler slid his arm around Adrienne's waist and planted a kiss on her cheek. She wouldn't make a fuss in front of her guests.

"You're absolutely gorgeous tonight," he whispered in her ear.

Tyler did it smoothly as though he had done it several times before. Peter and Simone looked on in open-mouthed surprise.

"Why, thank you, Tyler. That's very sweet of you."

"How do you two know each other?" Simone's features showed warmth toward Tyler. Her gaze shifted and she became her normal self again.

"Tyler, darling, it's so nice to see you." Hesitantly, Simone reached up and kissed him.

He returned the friendly gesture. He liked the woman and smiled at her. "Simone, you're as beautiful as ever."

"Thank you, Tyler." She smiled happily. She was pleased with his compliment and moved away to meet other friends.

Peter, in a cheerful mood, shook Tyler's hand. "Now that you're back, maybe we can get in a good bridge game."

"I'd like that. I'll give you a call," Tyler said.

"That will be great."

Tyler liked Peter. He wasn't a great player, but he enjoyed the game. Peter's wife had been seriously ill and died a few years before Adrienne left the island. Peter had taken it hard. He had an outstanding reputation as one of the island's leading cattleman and had been courting Adrienne before she met Steven.

"Are you going to spend some time with us?" Peter asked.

"I hope to spend the winter here," he responded.

"Good." Peter smiled, but his eyes remained watchful.

Tyler watched Adrienne's reaction to Peter. He wondered what she was thinking. He knew by Peter's attitude that he was still interested in Adrienne.

"I just like to be free when a project comes up. The renovations on the Lodge are completed and my home now."

"You enhance the landscape immensely." Another lady had joined the conversation.

"Thank you, Millie."

Tyler watched Adrienne as she talked with her grandmother's other guests. It all seemed friendly enough. Yet an undercurrent of uneasiness flowed through him.

Tyler moved back from the group. He shivered at the thought that someone in this room wanted Adrienne dead. It had entered his mind more and more in the last few days. He hadn't been able to shake it loose. There had to be more to the situation than he knew. He sensed undercurrents of pettiness and jealousies among the elite of the island.

"Darling, would you care for a drink? Please excuse us." Tyler took Adrienne's arm and led her from the group.

They left the guests chatting with other guests and made their way to the bar. Without asking Adrienne what she wanted, he ordered for her. When he returned, he handed her a drink of tonic water with a slice of lime.

He noticed the look on her face. "Are you surprised?"

"Yes, in a way, you seem to know a lot about my habits." She couldn't help smiling at him.

"Your grandmother checked me out. I did the same and found out about you."

"Did I meet all your expectations?" She looked full of mischief.

"Yes, and more. You're a beautiful woman. I'd like to see more of you."

"I believe there's more to it than that. There must be another reason, especially when you went to the trouble to find out about me."

His gaze was surveying the other guests. "First impressions are not the ones people should judge by." He smiled as he paraphrased her words.

They watched Simone as she charmed Adrienne's guests.

Adrienne noticed his look of dismay. "Simone's headstrong and self centered. My family spoiled her like the rest of us. Her mother, Alice, was a distant relative of my mother's. I seem to have a lot of distant relatives. She had fallen on hard times, and my father and mother believed in helping someone in need.

"Simone and her mother lived with us for a while. She worked for my father before she remarried and moved out, taking Simone with her. Simone wasn't happy about leaving Wyngate. We stayed friends even though we went different ways. To answer your unasked question, Simone always worries about the underdog and cares too much for the wrong people. She loved my brother. When he was killed, she took it very hard. Later she married, and, when her husband died, she inherited his ranch and was happy in the valley."

"I understand Peter's ranch is a showplace." Tyler remarked, changing the subject.

"A tour of the ranch is a must for visitors. It's one of the finest on the island."

Peter interrupted them. "I'm sorry, but it's getting late. Simone and I must leave. Darling, I'm glad you're home, and we must get together soon. I'll call you."

"That will be nice." She wasn't happy about Peter's offer but he was an old friend and she couldn't refuse.

Tyler watched as Alex arrived with a flourish of good wishes just before the party was breaking up. He went to Charlotte and gave her a bear hug, and he came over and did the same to Adrienne.

"Hello, Charlotte, Adrienne, love. Sorry to be so late, business always comes first."

Tyler knew Adrienne to be a true romantic. Her love for Charlotte, Alex, and the old house ran deep. Being away might have broadened her views, but her love would never diminish. People didn't stop loving something they've treasured all their lives, and yet a few people did give it up. They don't want the responsibility, no matter how big or small it was.

Soon, but not now, he hoped to convince Adrienne about his love for her and his reason for pursuing her. He wanted to unlock the mystery of the tragedies haunting her. He had to convince her that the family accidents were deliberate murder. There was a serial killer running loose. He hoped to prevent another "accident".

On his way back to Hunter's Lodge, Tyler turned and looked at Wyngate standing arrogantly against the moonlit night sky. Did Adrienne feel the same way about it now? The beauty had faded and was marred by old age and neglect. It was something the house couldn't help doing in her absence. Understanding Adrienne's reasons, he sighed. He knew heartache was a powerful demon. Would she still love and care for the house as much? Or, would she give it up freely without a backward glance?

What secrets did it hide behind that glorious and stiff-necked facade of old Southern architecture? Were the ghosts of Wyngates walking through those dark and lonely halls?

Chapter Twenty

The sky cleared and the stars shone in their glorious splendor. Tyler remained uneasy. He waited as Charlotte and Adrienne said goodnight to their guests. Adrienne stood in a glow of soft lights. She crossed the room with Alex and Charlotte out to the patio.

"Hello, Alex, glad you could make it." Tyler smiled at his friend.

"It's good to get away." Alex replied. The two men greeted each other like old friends.

"Let's move back into the house." Charlotte urged. Tyler agreed.

"We don't know who might be lurking in the bushes. What I want to talk about is for your ears only. Tyler, I know you don't accept many invitations. I was pleased you accepted mine for Adrienne's welcome home party."

"I wouldn't have missed it for the President."

"I didn't think you would."

They watched Charlotte with interest.

She turned to Tyler. "It's nice to know Hunter's Lodge will be occupied this season."

"Thank you. I'm glad to have a place to call home. The original plans were difficult to locate. I found them, and it made the job a lot easier for my workmen. The renovations are finally complete and I've moved in."

"You did a superb job on the house. It's back to its original splendor," Alex said.

"It has given me a great deal of satisfaction. I'm glad you approve. It's a shame more of them aren't restored," Tyler continued. "We're learning how important they are to the history of the island."

* * * *

Adrienne watched her grandmother. Usually, she was like a ballerina going through her paces, smooth and efficient, but tonight she was nervous. The fan in her hand clicked anxiously in the quiet that surrounded them.

"Hunter's Lodge isn't what you wanted to talk about," Charlotte said.

"No, it isn't." Tyler responded.

"You're here for a reason, and I'd like to know what it is. Are you looking for land to build a resort?" Charlotte asked.

"That's possible." Tyler's reply was evasive.

"Everyone knows there's little vacant land on Santa Isabella. Don't underestimate me." Adrienne challenged. "You've cultivated my friendship from the moment we met." She glared at Tyler. "Are you after Wyngate?"

"That's a good question. Unfortunately, I'm not ready to give you an answer at this time. I know Charlotte had me investigated. When you read the report, were you surprised to learn I was everything I said I was?"

"No." Charlotte replied. "You have all the attributes of one who is accustomed to money and education. Your manners are beyond reproach."

"Yes, I meet all those characteristics. Like you, I make it my business to know as much as possible about those I associate with, especially if they have something I want," Tyler said.

"Wyngate isn't for sale. It's the only land around here large enough to suit your purposes," Adrienne responded.

"Adrienne would never sell." Charlotte was emphatic.

"She's been away for three years. The mainland is another world where lifestyles can change rapidly. Maybe she's tired of carrying the burden of Wyngate," Alex said.

How had Alex guessed her thoughts? She loved the old place, but it was costing more and more each year to maintain. What if she met someone who didn't want to live in a big old drafty house? What would she do then?

"How can you say that, Alex?" Charlotte was quick to defend

Adrienne. "She'll never sell the house."

"There may come a time when she'll have to make a decision," Tyler said. "Wyngate by the Sea is at least three-hundred years old, and time has taken its toll on the old lady."

"What are you trying to say?" Charlotte was upset.

"After the wedding fiasco, you sent her away. What did you fear?"

"I'm not afraid of anything." Charlotte's words weren't convincing.

"What are you implying?" Adrienne fidgeted at the direction the conversation was taking.

"What business is it of yours?" Charlotte snapped, angry. "Why are you so interested in Wyngate and my granddaughter?"

"You'd better tell them," Alex said. "They should know."

"Only what they need to know," Tyler almost whispered.

"Just what is that?" Adrienne demanded.

"It concerns the disappearances of your cousin Eric and Steven Forrester."

"Eric?" Charlotte exclaimed.

"What do you know about them?" Shocked, Adrienne stared at him.

"Steven left you a note telling you he was going back to his old love in the States. Didn't your stepmother also leave a note saying she was returning to France?"

"How do you know what was in the notes?"

"Didn't you think it was odd they spoke to no one face to face to say they were leaving?"

"Yes, it was strange. It wasn't like them at all." Adrienne was stunned to hear her own thoughts repeated.

"There was no other woman in Steven's life but you. You were the only woman he loved."

"How do you know?" She doubted his statements.

"Let's say I have a vested interest. Steven never returned to the mainland."

"What are you suggesting?"

"Steven disappeared some time after his bachelor party. He hasn't been seen or heard from since. Someone didn't want him to marry you and wanted him out of the way."

"If what you say is true, who would do such a thing?" She couldn't think straight to ask the right questions. The old hurt took over.

Alex took Adrienne's hands in his. "Honey, there's no reason for him to lie. I had my men check everything out. We all believe Steven was murdered."

Silence filled the room. Each one was lost in their own thoughts.

Adrienne got up and ran to the terrace, pulling the doors closed behind her. Her loud sobs could be heard inside. Deep in her heart she had already known Steven was dead.

"Oh, my God." Charlotte put her hand to her mouth to stop from crying out.

"We know of no reason why Steven was killed. The only link we have is Adrienne. We believe someone wants to kill her. Charlotte, you tried to keep her whereabouts secret. I think this series of accidents she's having has something to do with Wyngate and the legendary 'Dead Man's Gold.'"

Adrienne listened, trying to keep her emotions under control. She re-entered the room.

"You've learned a great deal about Adrienne," Charlotte remarked.

"I make it my business to know about the people who are important to me."

"How can Adrienne be important to you? You've just met her."

"She is the key to this whole affair. If Adrienne were to marry and have a child, he or she would inherit everything. Whoever is behind this doesn't want that to happen. There are too many unanswered questions surrounding the Wyngate family. I don't like unanswered questions, and I intend to find the answers."

They might not be the answers Adrienne wanted to hear or what she might have to do about them.

Charlotte turned to Alex. "You knew all about this and said nothing."

"I've known Tyler for many years, and I trust him."

"I never heard you mention him," she said, offended.

"I swore Alex to secrecy. Some of the work I do is highly confidential. My partner doesn't like any kind of publicity. I thought it better not to tell anyone until now, for your safety, as well as Adrienne's."

"Are we in danger?" Charlotte demanded.

"Your worst fears for Adrienne may come true," Alex cautioned. "We must take precautions to protect both of you."

"You're serious about what you're telling us."

"Yes. We know you're upset at learning these details. We're asking for your help. If we work together, we can prevent other incidents. Adrienne has already had two accidents and the gift of a spider since she's come home."

"We'll leave you now," Tyler said. "Alex and I have plans to make. Good night, Charlotte. Adrienne, I'm sorry if I deceived you."

A flicker of uncertainty flitted across Adrienne's face. The implications frightened her.

Tyler bent down to her. "I wish there was a better way to tell you about Steven. Alex and I agreed it best for you to know so you can be on the alert. I need your help."

She nodded.

* * * *

Tyler knew Charlotte's servants could be trusted, so he saw to it they also knew about the dangers. He rode with Alex back to the casino. They decided to let their plans wait until tomorrow when they would be rested and refreshed.

The humidity hadn't let the night coolness completely take over. A chill of uneasiness swept over Tyler. Whoever the culprit was, Adrienne's return home had made him move his schedule forward. He wondered if his interest in Adrienne had anything to do with it. The enemy wouldn't give up until the culprit got what was sought. He had an idea of what was wanted, but not the reason for it. He had to be right about his plans or a lot could go wrong. The person behind Adrienne's unhappiness was a serial killer, and her return home had set off a domino effect. He had to find out who wanted to kill her and why.

Chapter-Twenty-One

As Adrienne approached Wyngate, silence surrounded her, waiting. Wild clumps of bougainvillea, hibiscus, and azaleas crowded the area. She approached the house with some nervousness. She stuck the key in the door and a rusted squeaking sound greeted her. She pushed the door wide open.

Inside, a dank and musty smell enveloped her. Reaching over, she flicked on the lights. She stood a few minutes to catch her breath. The dimness of the lights, the staleness, and neglect gagged her.

The hall lights gave off little light. She felt spider webs entangle her like a fishing net closing around her. Sheets, once white, covered the furniture. The heavy coating of dust made her sneeze several times.

In the gloom, she heard a noise and turned to see a mouse scurry across the floor. There were always field mice in the house, and once there had been several cats to keep them under control.

Adrienne moved down the hall through the semi-darkness toward the staircase. She glanced at the closed ballroom doors on her left. To see her bedroom first would prepare her for what lay behind those doors.

She climbed the staircase where frayed, white-taffeta ribbons were almost nonexistent. The orchids and ferns had long since disintegrated into dust. All that was left were little nubs clinging to the shreds of ribbon hanging from the banister. The ugly memories of that day rose in her mind.

After what she heard at Charlotte's last night, she should have heeded Tyler's warning and not come to the house alone. Pride led her to fight her own battles. No matter how hard the fight, she wouldn't let her tormented memories overpower her.

Adrienne used the banister for support and didn't mind the dust clinging to her hands. She turned on lights as she made her way down the long hall to her bedroom. Apprehension now claimed every nerve in her body. Opening the door was too easy. She reached for the light switch.

Pale light flooded the room. Going over to the windows, she pushed the drapes aside, and checked the sill for smudges, but saw none. She pushed the window open with some effort and then opened the broken shutters to let in the sea breeze. She inhaled deeply.

Adrienne remembered a voice calling to her and shivered. She tried to enjoy the beautiful tranquil scene below, frightened of what might come next.

The Virginia Lady's old hulk, half-buried, still rested on the sandbar. No matter how many storms occurred, they never succeeded in dislodging her from her resting place.

Adrienne examined the door. It was easy to see the hinges were well oiled. The dust covers lay in a pile on the floor. The furniture showed no traces of dust.

These telltale signs indicated someone had been using her room. The bed was unmade. It looked as if it had been used for a lovers' rendezvous. Who and how did they get in? Why her room? She went into her dressing room. In the cedar closet, she pushed back the plastic-covered clothes to check on the hidden passage concealed in the back wall of her closest. The mechanism had been recently oiled. Moving around the big closet, she stumbled upon a pile of clothes. Hesitantly she reached down and pulled the mass of white cloth from the floor.

"Oh, my God," She recognized her wedding gown. Her beautiful gown had been ripped to shreds. Entangled in the material was her lace and ivory mantilla. Dirt-covered the pearls, and the white ribbons were tattered and gray. Someone had dragged their dirty shoes across it. She quickly dropped it on the floor. Who would mutilate such a beautiful gown? She didn't know, but she would make damn sure she found out. Her fury was just beginning to emerge when she turned to leave.

"Now," Tyler's voice startled her. "Will you believe your life is in danger? You shouldn't go off by yourself."

"How long have you been standing there?" She was so lost in the past she hadn't even heard him enter. "What are you doing here? How did you get in?" Still angry, she hadn't forgiven him for alarming her and Charlotte.

"Charlotte called me. She was worried. You've been gone a long time."

"She needn't have worried. There's nothing in this house that can hurt me."

"Are you certain about that?" he said sharply.

Her eyes grew wide at his question. She knew he was right. Her whole life had changed again. Nothing was the same.

She watched him as he scanned the room with watchful eyes. He didn't miss anything, including the white pile of material at her feet. Without saying a word he walked over and picked up the bundle. As he examined it, several loose pearls landed on the floor and rolled by his feet.

"This was your wedding gown?"

"Yes." Her words were barely audible.

"Whether you like it or not, Adrienne, someone is out to harm you, and it isn't me."

"You've been spying on me." She stared at him in dismay.

"No, just making sure nothing else happens to you."

"Is my life so important to you?"

"For reasons I can't discuss with you now, your life is very important to me. Whoever is using your house didn't expect you to return. They were careless in not covering their tracks and leaving so much evidence behind."

"You sound like a detective."

"In my business, there is always some investigating needed. I like to know the strength and weakness of my competitors."

"But your main purpose in pursuing me is to get Wyngate."

"Not necessarily. I want you more than I want Wyngate."

She looked at him in astonishment. Was he being honest with her?

"I'm interested in your ancestral home for the secrets it hides and not for the reasons you think."

"You aren't going to tell me the real reason."

"Now isn't the time."

"What kind of game are you playing?"

"I don't play games. Not when someone's life is at stake." The terseness in his voice assured her he was serious.

"I'm not sure about anything anymore, least of all you," she complained.

"You never need to fear me. I want to help you."

"Why do I need help?"

"You do, but you won't admit it. The Wyngate genes run rampant through your veins."

"This is an absurd conversation."

"I'd die before I would let anything happen to you." He was serious and his words frightened her.

"Who are you?"

"It doesn't matter who I am, as long as you trust me. Does anything matter when your heart tells you you've found the right person?"

"You're being ridiculous. I've only known you a week."

"Am I? You have a lot on your mind. We both know someone is getting into this house and pretending it's haunted to keep people away."

"There's no way into the house unless they have a key, and my grandmother has the only two."

"Keys can be copied. What about the cellars and the secret entrance by the big chimney. It's on the other side of the house and covered by bushes." A wry smile crossed his face.

"How do you know about that? My father had all the cellars and tunnels sealed after I was locked in one. You know all about me and my house."

"As I said before, I always like to know about the people with whom I'm dealing. I know everything about you from the day you were born, your life at Wyngate, and what you did in the States."

"I don't believe you."

"You will, my dear." He was challenging her.

"Don't be too sure of yourself." She turned off the light, and he followed her down the hall to the gallery.

"Where are we going?"

"We are going to the Great Hall. Since you seem so interested in Wyngate, you might as well meet the rest of the family."

"From the rumors I've heard, it should be interesting."

"I'm sure it will be," she replied sarcastically.

Adrienne turned on the lights inside the gallery. The lights lit several portraits dating back to the seventeen hundreds. She didn't stop, but continued to the end of the room. She reached for a button and overhead lights lit up two fabulous gilt-framed portraits. Even after three hundred years, the colors were still rich and vibrant.

"Tyler, I would like you to meet Sir John Wyngate, the 'gentlemen pirate' and his wife, the Contessa Theodora. Johnnie and Theo are their nicknames. My great, great, great and how many more I don't remember, grandparents. They're the founders of the Wyngate family." She talked about them as though they were alive.

"My dear grandparents, I would like you to meet Tyler Prescott whom I know little about, although he thinks since my return, I need a protector."

"It's about time you arrived young man." Theo's eyelashes fluttered as she purred like a kitten.

Adrienne almost choked.

"All female Wyngates, no matter how strong they are, have always needed a man. The men are not to protect them, but to carry on the line. We have enough guts and brawn to take care of ourselves. Somewhere it is decreed we must marry and bring an heir to the family. Since her brother Elliot has passed over, it's up to Adrienne to bring the Wyngates an heir."

Tyler stared at the beautiful woman in the gold frame. He looked at Adrienne in disbelief.

"She has inherited all the good family genes and maybe a few not so good," Theo continued.

Tyler stared at Theo and then at Adrienne. He looked astonished.

"I've talked to them since I was a little girl," Adrienne explained. She shrugged it off as though it was nothing unusual.

"So you decided to return." Sir John still seemed miffed about her absence during the past three years.

"Grandmother Charlotte isn't well. I'm needed here."

"You didn't think of that when you left," he scolded.

"Things were different then. Charlotte insisted I leave."

"Just because you were left at the altar is not a catastrophe," Sir John thundered. "It's happened to many Wyngates."

"John, stop it," Theo reprimanded. "You will give Adrienne's young man a bad impression."

"He's not my young man," Adrienne corrected the Contessa.

"Oh? That's not the way it looks." Theo smiled, knowingly.

"Leave it to a woman to try her hand at matchmaking," Sir John retorted, sourly.

"Enough of this, John, Adrienne is home, and it's all that matters. She has a nice young man with her. It's a bonus."

"None too soon I might say." Sir John frowned while checking over Tyler.

"Why do you say that, grandfather?"

"Just be careful," he warned.

"Everyone's telling me to be careful," Adrienne muttered, exasperated. "No one says why."

"Young man, watch over her. She needs protection. Then…"Johnnie didn't finish his sentence.

"What do you mean?" Johnnie's unfinished statement puzzled Adrienne.

Tyler appeared surprised at Sir John and the Contessa. The old scalawag winked at Tyler and Theo flirted, saying nothing.

"Go, my children. The Contessa and I are tired. It's time for our siesta."

Adrienne turned off the lights. They made their way toward the main doors.

"I can't explain what we just saw and heard."

"Your ancestors are an interesting pair. They love you very much."

"They were quite tame this afternoon. At least they're glad to have me home."

"They're not the only ones." He took her hand in his.

She looked up and saw his smile. Before reaching the top of the stairs, she turned to him.

"Didn't you find it odd to see me talking to the portraits on the wall?"

"If you were telling me about it, I would not have believed you. I was there and witnessed it. No, I don't think it's odd to talk to your ancestors. I won't tell anyone your secret."

"You'd better not," she warned him. The odd feeling of being watched was overpowering.

Tyler stopped halfway down the steps.

"What's the matter?"

"I'm just chilly."

Had he also felt someone was watching them? The events of the last few days had made her more observant of her surroundings. She noticed Tyler walked without a limp.

"You're not limping today."

"It's one of my good days," he said as they descended the stairs.

He seemed so sure of himself in all his movements. She knew his infirmity wasn't an act. When he reached the bottom of the stairs, he turned to her. His face was in shadow and gave him a dramatic look. She was not afraid of him. His presence was reassuring. He seemed to be in no hurry to leave.

"Don't you have somewhere to go, like work or some meeting?" Adrienne said

"No. That's the fun of being your own boss. You can take off any time you want."

"You're the boss?"

"Yes, but I let everyone believe my partner is."

"But why?"

"I have my reasons. Don't ask any more questions. You'll get no answers," he teased.

A little twinge of jealousy from the night at Robert's overtook her. "Does Colette like you dropping in anytime?"

"Colette is my secretary. She's paid well for her work. Sometimes, she's a pleasant dinner companion."

"You don't have to explain."

"I want you to understand. You're the only woman in whom I'm interested."

"Sure, me and Wyngate."

Her nervousness showed as they approached the double doors to the ballroom. She tried pushing them open, but they wouldn't budge. Tyler put his shoulder to the doors and, with one solid push, the doors opened. Like most of the doors in the house they had warped from the dampness. She reached for the light switches. Dim lights from the chandeliers cast an eerie glow in the dark corners of the room.

Tyler followed her into the room and helped her open the windows and shutters. The light breeze scattered the dust mites as they floated through the open windows.

It was still a beautiful room. It once shone with the colors of white gold, coral, and blue. Dustsheets covered the furniture around the room. She knew the colors would be faded from the humidity.

Gifts that had been opened now showed tarnished silver and dull crystal. One large silver dish caught her eye. It had been Simone's gift to her and Steven. It was strange how their lives had taken different directions.

Adrienne made her way around the room, touching what was once beautiful crystal and silver, now marred by the passage of time.

On the guest tables the placards were faded and unreadable. They crumbled at her touch. With the heat, the candles in the floral pieces had melted down and left puddles of gray wax. In some places, the wax had spilled over onto the once white damask tablecloths.

A toppled bride and groom lay on the cake table. She remembered cutting the cake with an eagerness to be rid of it. The mice had a feast on the rest of it. Hard lumps of cake lay here and there. She swept her hand across the table, sending the china and crystal crashing to the floor. The glasses shattered. Silver twanged and the crashing of plates resounded through the empty room. She let pent up anger escape for what could have been. It was an emotion she could not control.

Tyler touched her arm. He gently turned her to him. "Adrienne, it's over. You can't have it back."

"I don't want it back. I've had enough pain." A sob escaped and uncontrolled tears flowed. She started to pound on his chest.

Tyler reached over and caught her hands. He pulled her into his arms. His eyes showed more than concern. It took a few minutes for her to calm down and regain her composure. Then he let her lean against him as her tears spread over his shirt.

"Is this the first time you've cried?"

"I've cried just one other time," she gasped between sobs.

"It's about time you got it out of your system." He pulled her closer. After awhile, she let him know she was coming to terms with the past. She moved out of his arms and away from him.

To her astonishment, he bowed and a bewitching smile crossed his lips. "May I have this dance, my Lady?"

"I'll be delighted, my Lord." She smiled and curtsied.

He led her to the dusty dance floor and swirled her around the room to the beat of music that only they could hear. They gazed into each other's eyes throughout the dance. Adrienne looked into dark brown pools of mystery, trying to fathom what he was thinking.

"Is your leg all right?"

"Don't worry. We'll see how long it'll hold up. You must have been a beautiful bride. I wish I could have been there to see you." He pulled her closer, burying his face in her hair, breathing in her perfume. Their hearts beat as one.

Adrienne wondered what there was about this man that attracted her. There was a magic she felt when she was with him. She still felt he was hiding a part of himself from her. Was he a great pretender wooing her so he could get Wyngate or was there another reason?

What did she fear? To take a chance again and find her love not wanted? She wanted to give freely the love that welled inside her. Yet, she found herself holding back. It was too soon, much too soon. They missed a step and stopped abruptly.

"Sorry. My leg is starting to give out." He let her go and bent down to rub the ache in his leg. He stood up and pulled her into his arms. Then he kissed her. Flames of desire wrapped her, and she returned his kiss with a passion she had long forgotten. His kiss flowed hotly through her.

"Cara Mia," softly spoken words sliced through her euphoria.

In one swift movement she moved away from him and stared. "Who are you? Why are you calling me 'Cara Mia'?"

Tyler swore under his breath. He had done it again. He smiled. "Those words are used quite often in different countries. It's Spanish. All it means is 'my dear'. Why did it upset you?"

"Steven always called me his 'Cara Mia.'"

"I'll try not to do it again." The smile left his face.

She saw his hurt and was upset. "If you're looking for the 'Dead Man's Gold', I hate to disappoint you. There's never been any proof it existed." She knew differently from Sir John, himself.

She didn't wait for an answer. She ran from the room and into the hallway where she tugged on the front door. When it opened, she ran into a surprised Peter.

Adrienne felt Peter's arms catch her to keep her from falling. He appeared surprised. "Adrienne, love, what's the matter?"

The voice of her old friend grated on her nerves. She recalled during the party last night there was none of the usual animosity between her friends. She thought it prudent not to mention Tyler's presence. Seeing Simone and Peter together, she thought what they didn't know was not any of their business anyway.

Tyler's attentiveness and the kiss had been unexpected and rocked her. She had kissed him back as though she had never been kissed before. Hunger for love had ignited a long dormant passion.

With Simone and Peter here, she didn't feel up to handling things. She loved her friends dearly and wanted to chat with Simone, but not now. Her thoughts were in turmoil.

They were friends she'd known all her life. Because of Tyler's warning, she wasn't sure if she could trust them. What was the matter with her? How was she going to keep from crying? Her reaction to being kissed, and the memories in the house of the wedding that never occurred, distressed her.

"Adrienne, what's happened?" Simone said. "You look like you've seen a ghost,"

Adrienne fidgeted and stumbled through her greeting. "Simone, Peter how nice to see you again."

She had seen a ghost, but he was very much alive. What really bothered her was this feeling of love for Tyler. She needed time to sort out her emotions.

"I'm sorry, seeing the old house brought back too many memories. They upset me more than I expected. It's good to see you again. How's everything at the ranch?"

"I can't complain. There's always more work than I need. It takes a lot of effort to keep my ranch in prime condition," Simone replied.

"You're looking more gorgeous then ever." Peter said as he sized Adrienne up with that wanton look.

She was glad she had refused his offer of marriage. A frisson of ice crawled up her spine at his piercing look, leaving her chilled. He still wanted her. There was a hardness about her friends she had never noticed before.

Adrienne tried to change the conversation to something else. It didn't deter Simone. She reached in her purse and took out a clean handkerchief.

"Here, wipe your face." Simone handed the small piece of linen cloth to her. Adrienne felt like a little child being scolded. She was surprised not to see a closed fan in her friend's hand. She often used it to tap someone's shoulder lightly to get attention. Adrienne remembered her friends liked the finer things in life.

"It's the first time you've been in the house since you returned. I can see how it would upset you." A touch of sympathy came from Simone.

If Simone knew what upset Adrienne, she would have a fit and wouldn't be showing her kind side. Simone liked her men to be picture perfect. Tyler was definitely not to her liking.

"Yes, seeing the house and the condition it's in upset me." She would use it as an excuse and go on to something else. "Living on the ranch in the valley seems to agree with you, Simone."

"It is. Living in the valley is great. I found a good ranch foreman, well recommended, and he does a great job. He's a bachelor and also quite handsome."

Adrienne saw the look in Peter's eyes and gathered he didn't like the man.

"She hired him without checking his references," Peter complained.

Adrienne had already heard about it and didn't inquire further. The man was trustworthy and did a good job. What difference did it make? Why was Peter upset? Simone was old enough to make her own decisions. Adrienne was beginning to think there were some underlying aspects of this conversation she was missing.

Peter liked money, and she wondered if he had wanted to court Simone now that she was wealthy. Maybe this foreman was more than just a foreman. Adrienne decided it was none of her business.

The conversation continued. Adrienne, facing the forest of trees, listened half-heartedly to Simone and Peter rattle on about the latest social activities at the country club. She had no interest in any of it. She still hadn't recovered from Tyler's kiss.

Peter walked methodically back and forth across the lawn, giving the impression he was looking for something. What made her think of the gold? He probably had a lot on his mind and was just lost in thought.

"What do you think of Tyler Prescott, our new boy wonder?" Simone's question had an unfriendly tone to it. Something in the way she spoke irritated Adrienne.

"I really don't know the man that well."

She wasn't about to let her friend know the very man they were talking about had kissed her. He had sent shock waves up and down her spine and was inside her house at this moment.

"You seemed quite friendly at your grandmother's the other night."

Simone was fishing for information and Adrienne wasn't about to satisfy her curiosity.

"I just met the man and have no idea what he's like."

"That's not what I heard," Simone said coyly.

"What did you hear?"

"I heard he sent you your favorite orchids. He dropped his date with Collette to bring you home after you fell at Robert's. He's rich and eligible. He wants Wyngate. Darling, you know the island survives on gossip."

Adrienne looked at her friend. "You should know better then to gossip." She was offended that Simone would listen to such rumors.

"He's been seen with Collette quite a few times. She supposedly works for him."

What was Simone trying to tell her? So what if Tyler dated other women. She was curious about Simone's information. "I thought Collette was married."

"She is. Her husband's not able to work so she has to. It's common knowledge they both fool around."

Adrienne didn't like Simone's insinuations. "The times I've encountered Tyler Prescott, he was quite personable."

"I still wouldn't trust him. Nobody knows anything about him. Why

Charlotte is taking an interest in him is beyond me. I think he's dangerous."

"Why say a thing like that when you hardly know the man? I find him interesting and knowledgeable."

"What if he's after your money and Wyngate? After all, you're the richest woman in the islands."

Was this Simone's way of warning her? Was she afraid she would lose Adrienne's friendship if she married? She turned away, not wanting Simone to see her feelings for Tyler.

Peter wandered back and rejoined them. "When are we going to get together, love?"

"Anytime you want. Just call and we'll set a date."

"Is tomorrow night a good time for you?"

"What time?" She saw the look on Simone's face and wondered why Simone looked so concerned? Was she upset because Peter was asking her out?

She glanced over toward the trees and saw a movement in the bushes on the far side of the yard. Someone was watching them. If it was Tyler, she would give him a piece of her mind. He wouldn't do anything like that or would he? Maybe he thought he was protecting her. Everybody else seemed to want to do the same thing. Protect her from what?

The movement was so subtle. Some bushes swayed in the breeze.

Peter looked anxiously at his watch. "I hate to rush you, Simone. I do have an appointment at the ranch."

"Sorry, Peter, I forgot. Adrienne, it's so good seeing you again. You'll have to come out to the ranch and see all the improvements we've made."

"I'd like that." Adrienne wondered who the 'we' was, but said nothing.

"Good, I'll give you a call. Bye, darling."

Adrienne watched Simone and Peter walk down the driveway toward the gates. Deep in her heart she wished her friends much happiness. They left through the small gate in the wall next to the main gate. She waited until she heard Peter's car drive away and went over to the bushes where she had seen movement. No one was there. Was Tyler sneaking around, listening to her conversations? She thought not. Yet someone had been there.

She walked up the steps and opened the door. A fleeting memory overtook her. When she ran away from Tyler, she had no trouble opening the front door. It had been unlocked. How could that be? She hadn't had time to unlock it.

She stared at the door for a minute. On entering the house, she listened and looked around the front hall. Hearing nothing, she took the key out of her pocket and locked it. Where was Tyler? Had he left, believing she'd be a long time with her friends?

"Tyler. Where are you? Tyler?" Her words echoed around the entrance hall. "They're gone. You can come out now."

"He's not here." A smooth low rhythmic voice answered, startling her. It wasn't the voice she expected to hear, but she was happy to hear it.

Chapter Twenty-Two

Hannah stood silhouetted against the ballroom doors. Her multi colored muumuu had blended in nicely with the foliage outside. Her height and build were statuesque, belying her sixty-odd years. Sparkling brown eyes shone brightly in a pecan-colored face, and her pearly white teeth were like her grandson's, Trinidad. He had inherited his grandmother's good qualities.

Her dark beauty made her the most beguiling priestess on the island, a title she shrugged off. In her younger days she was one of the first women to attend medical school and graduate with high honors. After acquiring some experience on the mainland, she came back to the island to look after her people. She was the islander's main medicine woman. She worked for the Wyngates to earn money to buy medicine and the things needed for her people.

"You were in the bushes listening."

"Of course. How else can I learn things? I've missed you." There was no preamble to her words, just straight forward and to the point. "Your grandmother told me you'd be here. She's very happy you're back."

"And you?" She looked at the woman she had known all her life.

"Child, it was time for you to come home."

"Is my being home going to make a difference?"

"Yes. Your coming home is making a difference. Come, let's sit down in the ballroom. Memories, whether they are good or bad, are nothing to fear. Or is it what happened between you and Tyler earlier today that bothers you?" She looked at Adrienne. "No, I don't think so. In fact, I think you were surprised and pleased he's interested in you."

110

Warmth flooded Adrienne's face.

"So, you did like it." Hannah chose a table near the back of the room. It didn't seem possible that Hannah was almost the same age as her grandmother and yet her hair was as black and shiny as a horse's newly brushed coat.

Adrienne watched as Hannah picked up the tablecloth by its four corners and deposited it and its contents on another table. The top was clear of any impediments. They sat down, and Hannah laid her hands across the table while reaching for Adrienne's. Her pale hands were a contrast to Hannah's soft brown fingers and lacquered nails.

Hannah closed her eyes and held Adrienne's hands for several minutes before speaking. "You have had much trouble in your young life, and there is more to come. There is much danger ahead for you."

"I don't like the way that sounds. How much danger is there?"

"We think quite a bit. You must learn to trust Tyler even though you don't think you should. He wants you more than Wyngate." Her words surprised Adrienne.

"What do you know of Tyler Prescott?"

"He has been hurt like you and hides many secrets."

"So, I'm not the only one who thinks he's hiding something."

"I wouldn't worry about it. A time will come when you'll have no secrets from each other. You have other things to worry about. This house weighs heavily on your mind. It's been a burden on your shoulders too long."

"You've been talking to my grandmother."

"We talk, but not about these things. Charlotte is a great keeper of secrets."

"You read Charlotte's mind like you do mine." Adrienne smiled at her.

"That is true." Hannah smiled back.

"Yet, you aren't scolding me for thinking of it."

"The time is coming when you will not have to worry about Wyngate."

"Not even with the gold and its ghosts?"

"Even if there's no gold, the legend makes life more interesting."

"I know. I worry about it all."

"Stop worrying. You've made your decision. You want another Christmas in the old mansion. The decision will no longer be yours."

"What are you saying? It will no longer be mine."

"I see nothing past the New Year. I can't tell you more. You will have your Christmas holidays and much more."

"I want it to be the way my mother and father had it when they were alive. The house gaily decorated with presents under the tree. I almost forgot the crèche and manger sitting in the curve of the stairway. I want an old fashioned Christmas with the Masquerade Ball and fireworks on New Years Eve."

When she looked back at Hannah she saw a puzzled look on her face. Hannah quickly pulled her hands away, breaking contact.

"Is something wrong?"

"No, the idea overwhelms me." She fumbled for words. "I think it's a great idea. The house will go out with a bang."

Adrienne watched Hannah's face. It revealed nothing, and she wondered what the woman wasn't telling her.

"If, you want to do all these things for Christmas, there is no time to lose. The holidays are almost here."

"Then we must inform my grandmother at once and start to work getting a cleaning crew in here immediately."

"I'll take care of that. There are evil forces working against you. They will not win. You have more than one protector. There's a difficult time ahead for you, so be careful. It will be some time before the storm around you clears and gives you a freedom and love you have never known." In a way, her words sounded ominous.

"I think I can handle anything that comes along. I have so far and intend to do so in the future." Adrienne got up from the table and went over to kiss Hannah on both cheeks.

"Thank you, Hannah."

"You're welcome, my dear. I'll have a work crew in here tomorrow."

"Won't some of the natives be squeamish about working in a haunted house?"

"You have been away too long. You should know money always soothes a superstitious soul."

Chapter Twenty-Three

Tyler berated himself for making such a blunder. Adrienne had run from his arms and didn't want anything to do with him. He would have to find a way to correct his mistake. Maybe it was just as well. He wasn't able to keep his hands off her. The more he saw of her, the more he wanted her. He'd need all the control he could muster in the next few weeks.

He rubbed his leg. The damn thing would have to bother him now. He bent down and rubbed it for a bit and then moved upstairs. He watched the scene below him from one of the front bedroom windows.

Adrienne greeted her friends Simone and Peter. He thought Peter held her close a little too long. Pangs of jealousy pierced him. Charlotte must have told them Adrienne was here. They sat down on one of the old wrought iron benches under the big magnolia tree on the front lawn. He suspected Adrienne wouldn't mention his presence. He thought she was beginning to like him, and yet, he sensed and saw a wariness in her attitude. He had undone what he had accomplished by uttering those words. He would have to be more careful in the future.

He watched Adrienne and her friends for several minutes and then moved on. He didn't want her to come back and find him rummaging through her room and the bedrooms.

He went into another bedroom and looked out the window. Adrienne and her friends were still sitting on the bench talking. He came away and surveyed the room. It had been dusted recently. He went on to the next room. He examined each one carefully looking for telltale signs of occupancy. Adrienne's room was the only one that showed any evidence of having been used.

The furniture was shrouded in sheets that had once been white and now were covered with a gray layer of dust. Shutters covered the windows and gave just enough light for him to see his surroundings. This one must have been her brother's room. It had the style of a young man. Faded ship and plane posters covered the walls.

It was getting cloudy from what he could see through the shutters. He didn't think it would be wise to use his flashlight in the front rooms of the house with Adrienne and her friends below. Adrienne would be occupied for a while, talking over old times. He returned to Adrienne's bedroom and examined it methodically, inch by inch feeling, pressing, pushing anywhere he thought there might be an entrance to a secret passage. It took some time for him to discover a small rosette in the design high above the mantle. He pressed the center of the flower and it exposed a hidden passage.

It made a soft shushing sound as quiet as a whisper. The runners on the door were well oiled indicating that someone had recently used this entrance. He didn't discover any other signs of use. He went inside and saw there was just enough light to see the passage went to the left and turned right again after several feet. Dirt and cobwebs clung to the sidewalls. The area was stuffy and made him sneeze. A mouse, awakened by his presence, scampered across the floor.

He stopped to catch his breath and rest his leg. Damn, it hurt more. That's what he got for overdoing it by dancing. It was nice holding Adrienne in his arms and he couldn't regret that.

The floor beneath him was uneven in places, but clean. There were no footprints to follow. He had no idea where the passageway would lead him. He was determined to find out.

There were eight bedrooms on the second floor of the house and each had a peephole where one could watch the guests romping and any other activities in which they might indulge.

Sir John and Theo must have enjoyed the bedroom antics of their guests. Tyler searched the walls for any indications of where he was in the house when he spotted a larger peephole. The family gallery of portraits appeared before him. It was a different angle making the portraits look ominous. The eyes of the pirate and the Countess glowed with mischief. He surveyed the room.

"Push the button on the right, you naughty boy," Theo coaxed. "It will open a panel, and you can come out."

Tyler found the button and pushed. He stepped out of the darkened passageway and brushed himself off. He stood and faced the portraits.

"There you are, my dear man. We heard you fumbling around back there."

"You did? I thought I was being very quiet."

"You were, but we have very sensitive hearing."

"He has learned our secret. What are we going to do?"

"Johnnie, at times you can be so oafish. We're not going to do anything."

"You need not worry, Contessa, your secret is safe with me." He suspected that they did more than just watch. It would add a bit of spice to the rumors of old.

"Have you found what you are looking for yet?" the Contessa said.

"I'm still looking."

"Good luck, you will need it," Sir John responded coolly.

He bid them goodbye and returned to the passageway. The house had been unoccupied for several years. These passages should be covered with cobwebs and they weren't. He saw mice running about. Nothing was as dusty as it should be. Adrienne's room was dust free as though someone had just cleaned it.

After returning to the passageway, he came across a flight of steps that led downward. He carefully played his light over them to make sure there were no broken steps and nothing to hinder his way. Descending the stairs, he found the passage branched off to his right, and he assumed it covered the first floor. What lay at the bottom of the steps interested him more.

He counted thirteen steps down and came to a small landing and a blank wall. The cold and dampness seeped into his bones and he shivered. He should have worn a jacket, but it would have looked out of place on such a hot day. The outline of what had once been a door stood out. The door had been plastered over. Old pieces of debris lay scattered on the floor. Someone evidently didn't like it being closed. It had been reopened. There was no handle. Tyler grunted as he pushed his weight against the door. After pushing a few times he moved his weight to one side of the door. It moved in on its side as though the door was on an axis. With a heavy push, it swung around giving him enough space to squeeze through.

The room he entered had no footprints. The air was stagnant. The smell of decay was prominent. He played his light around. It was some kind of storeroom. Against one wall were dirt-covered boxes marked Christmas. He remembered at one time Wyngate had been known for its festive Christmas and New Year parties.

He searched the room. Behind the boxes, he found a narrow door in the wall and carefully opened it. He found himself in the wine cellar. Row upon row of bottles covered with grime lined the shelves. The only bottles that were clean were sitting on a shelf by themselves and an empty glass stood next to them. The intruder was making himself at home.

How did he get in? Whoever it was, knew his way around the house.

He carefully scouted the room for any other signs of use and soon discovered the room had its own refrigeration unit, keeping the wine at the right temperature. That alone would cost the estate a pretty penny. Who might be enjoying Adrienne's wines and her home at her expense? He moved toward the main door of the room and carefully opened it onto a wide dead end passage. He returned the way he came and followed the other passageway, which led him into a large storage closet with a door opening into the kitchen. He looked around at the tarnished pots and pans hanging from the ceiling and the large work counter. The stoves were large and of a type one found in restaurants. Any chef could work to his heart's desire in this kitchen. It had everything.

Retracing his steps, he was back at the wall. One look at the stone walls and ceiling told him he was inside one of the rooms that had been carved out of the cliffs centuries ago and made into storerooms for stolen goods captured by Gentleman John and his crew of pirates. Tyler had heard the legend of how Gentleman John had captured a Spanish Galleon, kidnapped the Viceroy's wife, and a fortune in gold. Sir John settled down for good with the Contessa and raised two sons and a daughter. It was a strange love match.

Tyler tried several other doors without being able to open them. He thought that age may have rusted the hinges and would yield to his strength, but none did. He would need some sturdy tools to break open the heavy sealed doors. Odd that these doors were made of iron. He would need time to explore and be better prepared. What he expected to find would not be a treasure.

Chapter Twenty-Four

"You're fired."

The words echoed in Collette's head. She sat at the bar drinking her fourth Martini. She felt stupid for letting Mr. Madison catch her going through Tyler's desk. Careless was the word she should have used. She would have to tell her husband. He'd be furious because it meant he would have to give up Marcella, his lover. She wouldn't like the idea of not being paid.

When she arrived home, her husband was sitting on the couch. He had a glass of whiskey in one hand, and a bottle sat on the floor. From the expression on his face, she could tell he was drunk and in pain. She was in no mood to listen to his whining about how bad life had treated him.

"So, you finally decided to come home," he growled.

"What difference does it make to you if I'm home or out?" she yelled back.

"It doesn't. Where's my money?" he demanded.

"You have all the money you're going to get from me."

In one swift movement he pushed himself out of his chair and swung his fist into her face. "I want my money," he shouted.

It was the first time he had hit her in the face. The other times he hit her in places that didn't show. Her jaw hurt, but she didn't scream from the pain. She wouldn't let the bastard have the satisfaction of knowing he'd hurt her.

"They must have paid you something. Give it to me," he spat. "Do you think your lover will want you when there's no money?"

"It doesn't matter," she hollered back. Insults again.

She moved close to him. "He loves me."

Her husband's high pitched, uncontrolled laughter echoed through the house.

She had taken enough of his abuse. In her brain something snapped. Her fury rose as she picked up the bottle and swung it with all her force, hitting him in the temple. He fell backwards onto the floor screaming with pain. She bent over and continued hitting him. All the hate she had stored up over the years broke loose. Her eyes glazed over as she watched him struggle, enjoying every minute of his agony. She hit him again, hard.

"Help me. Collie. Help me."

She answered his pleas by hitting him again. This time he didn't move. She had killed him.

The fury inside her reached a fever pitch. She saw the bloody pulp of what was once her husband's face. The bottle still in her hand, she walked into the bathroom. She washed and wiped the bottle clean and then tidied herself. Sober faced, she went back into the room. She took what money he had in his wallet and shoved it in her bag. Still not feeling clean, she returned to the bathroom, undressed, and took a shower.

After the shower, she dressed in her lover's favorite tee shirt and shorts. He liked easy access to her body. She was looking forward to this evening and the kinky sex they would have.

At her dressing table, she carefully applied her makeup. She experienced no feelings of regret or sorrow, only a sense of relief. Laughter bubbled inside her. At last she was free and could be with her lover forever.

* * * *

That evening, Collette parked her car next her lover's beat up brown truck under a grove of trees. It hid them from the main road. Her lover was already here. He didn't like her being late. Tonight was going to be different. She was going to assert herself and demand a few things instead of always doing what he wanted. Yes, tonight was going to be different.

The stillness of the dark and foggy night made her nervous. The trees whispered to each other. It sent cold chills down her back. She found her way from the grove to the driveway. No moon shone to guide her to the house, leaving her with an eerie feeling. What she had to tell her lover would make him mad, but she knew how to handle him.

She went through the side gate and slowly made her way up to the Wyngate Manor. Inside, so she wouldn't fall, she counted the steps into the house and up the spiral staircase. The house was too quiet. She made her way down the hall to Adrienne's bedroom. A smile turned up the corners of her mouth at the thought of using Adrienne's room for their trysts.

Why should she care about Adrienne? Collette liked the idea of sleeping on silk sheets even if they weren't her own. When would she ever have the money to own silk sheets?

They always suspected the spouse first in a murder. She'd just pretend she was with a lover. Her lover was single and had money. Fucking never bothered her before and wouldn't bother her now, even if he was married. Why shouldn't she have some of the gravy too?

The house rightfully belonged to her lover, and someday she would be Mistress of Wyngate. Tonight, she had proven that revenge was indeed sweet.

She knocked twice softly and waited for an answer.

"Come in." As usual his voice was warm and welcoming.

In the dim candlelight, she could hardly see him. He was bare, all except for the mask he always wore when they were together. Tonight she was determined to find out who he was. His silken suntanned body lay stretched across the bed, waiting.

Not wearing any undergarments she found it easy to strip as she made her way across the dimly lighted room. She leaned over him and splayed her body over his, rubbing herself against him. She smothered him with kisses.

Chapter Twenty-Five

"You've been drinking again." He pushed her away and sat up. He didn't like drunks, especially women, but as long as she worked for Tyler Prescott, she was of some use to him.

"I have a right to have a few drinks after what happened today." Her eyes glittered with excitement.

What had she been doing? He reached over to the bedside table and poured himself a drink. Collette reached for the glass and he pulled it away, downing it in one swallow. Then, he reached for her. First, he wanted to know anything new she had learned, and then she could have a drink. She was easy to handle, and he knew how to please her. However, tonight he had other plans for her.

He changed his mind and decided against waiting to let her have a drink. It would loosen her up and make her talk. He poured her a stiff drink, larger than the one he had and watched her gulp it down.

"Oh, that tastes so good. Can I have another one?"

He poured her drink and she curled up next to him. He wanted her loose and pliable. Her hands were shaking and the whiskey dribbled onto her chest. He sensed what she was going to tell him would have a profound effect on their future relationship.

Collette was drunk and he could do anything he wanted to with her. When she got this way, he had no problem tying her spread eagle across the bed. He grasped her breasts and squeezed the nipples hard.

"Oh, darling, do it again," she cooed, drunkenly.

An obliging lover, he did it again, knowing how much she liked it. Her moans gave way to shrieks of pain, sending her into sheer ecstasy.

"Don't stop. Just keep doing it. It sends me spiraling out of control."

Again, she cried out for more. He did as the 'lady' wished. Lady was an odd word to apply to a slut who excited him. She would lay with any man who was willing to pay. Her husband was just as bad. Luckily, he found both liked quirky sex, and that information, along with some other material he gathered about them, helped add to his income. He always needed money.

He shoved her down on the bed and sprawled over her. His hands slid up and down her naked body, provoking her to the heights of passion. Then, he tied her to the bed and entered her hard. He had no mercy. She cried out for more.

His prickly hair rubbed against her body. She acted as if she had died and gone to heaven. She was a greedy bitch, always wanting more. Again, he entered her hard and fast without any foreplay. She bucked and reared like a bronco. She cried out as he drove in deeper and deeper.

"Oh, baby, you're terrific." The words were hardly audible among her cries of passion.

He untied her and taking her head in his hands kissed her. "Now, darling, don't you think it's time you told me what happened today."

She started to laugh, feeling slightly giddy. "I can't give you any more money."

"What do you mean?" He waited for more.

"I was fired. I got caught in Tyler's office going through his files."

"Fired? That wasn't very smart."

His eyes turned cold. He wouldn't lose his temper with her just yet. Not until he knew all the details.

"I was fired." She shrank back as she said the words. She saw his scowling look.

"Did you learn anything?"

He didn't give a damn about her personally, but he needed to know about Tyler Prescott and what he was doing. He pushed her away from him. Getting up from the bed, he moved around the room.

"What else happened? Don't lie to me. I always know when you do."

She started to shake. He came over and took her in his arms, holding her close.

"You might as well tell me. You know I always find out." Then he saw the bruise on her face. "Has your husband been hitting you again?"

He sat in a chair and pulled her down to the floor where she had to look up at him. She saw the grim look and shrank back.

"He won't do it anymore," she sobbed.

"What won't he do any more?"

He doubted he was going to like what she had to tell him. She hesitated and tried to bury her head in his lap. He saw no tears. Maybe she had finally left her husband.

She looked up at him clear eyed and without remorse. "I killed him," she said. "He taunted me about getting fired." Shudders racked her, and she couldn't stop.

"You killed him?" he said, amazed.

"With the whiskey bottle. Once I started hitting him, I couldn't stop. The bastard got everything he deserved. He's lying in a puddle of blood on the den floor."

Her confession floored him. He never thought she'd be so stupid. She was messing up his plans, and the only way to solve the problem was to...

"Did anyone see you leave your house?"

"I wiped my prints off everything, including the bottle, and came here."

"That wasn't very smart."

"I made sure no one saw me."

"Well, it doesn't matter. We can't use this place much longer. Adrienne's planning to reopen the house."

He moaned when she moved her head. She was raising hell with his body parts.

"What will we do?"

"You needn't worry, my dear."

She was moving her head back and forth against his organs making him hard, very hard. She was in such glorious abandonment. She didn't see him put on a pair of gloves. He moved her head so that she could take him in her mouth. Her moans of ecstasy vibrated through him. If nothing else, she did a good blow job. The torment of passion roared through him as his body convulsed.

Exhausted she rested her arms on his thighs. He gently removed them so they hung down close to her body, between his legs. She let his shaft slip out of her mouth to catch her breath. She looked up at him in pure delight, obviously hoping she had pleased him.

"Didn't I please you?"

He didn't answer her and sneered.

"What's wrong?"

As he shoved a scarf in her mouth, she tried to scream. He squeezed her body tightly between his legs, knocking the breath out of her. He crossed his ankles so she couldn't move. She didn't fight, perhaps hoping he was making up a new game for them to play.

"You're no longer of any use to me. Did you think I would tie myself to a drunken slut like you?"

Collette struggled, and the more she fought, the tighter he held her. He tightened his grip around her throat, squeezing the last breath out of her. He laughed as her body relaxed.

At first, she had been a good lay and a means to get the information he wanted. Now, she was no longer any use to him. He had no intention of making her mistress of Wyngate. His laughter rose from his throat as he let her limp body fall to the floor.

He liked the look of surprise on her face when he started to squeeze the life out of her. He enjoyed killing. This was the first murder he had done since he killed Francine many years ago. The urge had been growing for some time, and she was the perfect subject. It was good preparation for the time when he married Adrienne and became master of Wyngate Manor, his rightful home.

He pushed Collette's body aside with his foot. He got up and dressed, packing the few things that would link him to the room in his briefcase. When he was satisfied there was nothing to connect him to the house, he reached down and hefted Collette's limp body over his shoulder and disappeared into the hidden passageway. This way he would meet no one, and, if necessary, he could leave her body in the cave. Like the others, it wouldn't be found for years, if ever.

After gaining entrance to the storeroom, he dropped her in a heap with the others. After all everyone, even in death, needed company. His laughter echoed through the room.

Chapter Twenty-Six

Adrienne, half asleep, picked up the ringing phone to hear Charlotte's' voice.

"Have you seen this morning's paper?" her grandmother said.

"I'm afraid not. You woke me." She swept the sleep from her eyes.

Adrienne sat up. "What's so special about it?"

"Stanley Brewster, Collette's husband, was murdered last night, and Collette is missing."

"Do they have any idea who did it?" Adrienne said. "I heard they weren't getting along. Maybe she got caught fooling around one too many times."

"They were never the ideal couple. There were rumors. I understand she was as bad as he was. After his boating accident, he drank a lot, and she had to work to support them."

"She was with Tyler the night I fell at Robert's."

"I know. Tyler had taken her out to dinner a few times. I think the only reason he did was because he felt sorry for her."

"How do you know that?"

"Tyler gave her a job because Peter asked him to do it. He figured if she had a paying job, it would straighten her out."

"He's a good Samaritan." It didn't surprise Adrienne. "Do you think he might be involved?"

"Oh, goodness no. Stanley wasn't an easy man to live with even before his accident."

Adrienne mulled this over. She had known the Brewsters slightly. Collette loved to drink and party and had gone through her inheritance. Adrienne had heard she couldn't hold a job for any length of time.

Charlotte interrupted her thoughts. "I'm meeting Jolie for lunch at her place. Why don't you join us?"

"Love to. I have some errands to do first. Later this afternoon, I'm going up to the house. George is meeting me there to discuss what needs to be done."

"I'm glad you're going to use him."

"It's not because he's family, well partly that. He's good at what he does."

"Have you been to his shop yet?"

"No. I intended to stop by this afternoon."

"Well, he has a new assistant, a lovely lady from Bermuda."

"Ooh?"

"He's very much in love with her."

Adrienne was glad to hear her cousin had found someone. She was happy for him. She had the feeling she should change the subject. He was a distant relative her father had taken care of after his parents were killed in a boating accident.

Charlotte hadn't approved of George's parents' Bohemian life style, and the way they raised him. He was an artist and a bit eccentric. When he returned from his wanderings, he settled down and opened an interior decorating business. He had made a success of it. Her grandmother had disapproved of George from the beginning, but seemed to be softening in her feelings for the man who had been young and arrogant.

"I have decided to reopen Wyngate for the holidays."

"Oh darling, Hannah called and confirmed my suspicions that you would. Do you think it's wise? Why are you going to so much expense for just a few weeks?"

"It might not be just for the holidays. I'm serious about living there again. I hope you'll move back in with me."

She expected a response, but received none. It surprised her because she thought her grandmother would vigorously object.

"The house has been empty too long. It needs some loving care," she continued.

From what she saw the other day, it would need a lot of care. She intended to give it just that, by refurbishing and bringing it back to life.

"Adrienne, you have always treated the house as a person, and I know you love it, but …"

"I want to have a Christmas holiday and New Year's Ball like we used to have when Mom and Dad were alive." She intentionally cut her grandmother off. "I want a big tree with lots of ornaments, the Masquerade Ball, and fireworks. A fresh pine tree brought in from the mountains and candles will be used to light the mansion, just like it was in the olden days."

"My dear, candles are so dangerous," Charlotte warned.

"Hannah believes they can have the house ready. Remember how you used to enjoy the holidays."

"Aren't you overdoing it?" Charlotte's unease with her plans was troubling.

"It's something I feel I must do." Adrienne thought of past Christmases and the manger scene. Her mother and father always arranged it in the space under the staircase. How strange, she should remember it now.

"Do you know where the manger is?"

"It's probably packed away with all the other Christmas ornaments and decorations in one of the storerooms below the house."

She would have to get the old ornaments out, go through them, and see what else was needed. She had a long list of chores to do. She didn't mind. It would keep her busy and her mind off Tyler.

"What time are you meeting Jolie?"

"Can you make it about one o'clock?"

"I'll be there," Adrienne said.

"See you then. I love you."

"Love you, too."

With all that was happening, her grandmother would worry. She put the phone back in its cradle and went to shower and dress.

Chapter Twenty-Seven

It was such a beautiful day. Once in town, Adrienne decided to park at Jolie's place and walk to her lawyer's office. She received a monthly report on the status of Wyngate Enterprises. It revealed she had more than enough money to renovate her ancestral home.

Earlier, Adrienne had called the family lawyer and told him what she wanted. She entered their modern offices to be greeted by Mrs. Alcott.

"Miss Wyngate, it's so good to see you again. Mister Rooney has the papers ready for you."

Adrienne followed her into an office. Mr. Rooney had been the family attorney for many years, just as his father had before him. His sons would carry on after him. The heavy-set man rose and came around his desk to take her in his arms.

"Well, my dear, it's good to see you're looking so chipper."

"I'm feeling great and it's good to be home."

"Missed this old codger, did you?"

"Of course, I did."

"We took care of the bequests you wanted. Are you sure you want to do this?"

"For now, it's for the best. I've had a few mishaps since my return, and another might become fatal. My estate will be in order."

"Adrienne, you're not serious?" He turned pale. "Who would want to hurt you?"

"Yes, I'm serious. I have no idea who it could be."

"You take care and be careful."

"Thank you for all your help and have a nice day."

She felt much better now that her will was settled. With the holidays coming, they had worked overtime to get it done for her.

After leaving the lawyer's office, Adrienne wanted to stop by Dana's to have her hair styled and get a massage. It would do until she had time to make a regular appointment. Dana's Salon was located in the center of Old Town in the Brick Palace. It was surrounded by smart boutiques and shops.

Adrienne left Dana's with a new hairstyle that made her feel as if she could conquer the world. Suddenly, a prickling sensation at the back of her neck struck. Looking around, she didn't see anyone who looked remotely interested in her. She tried to relax, but the feeling of uneasiness stayed with her. The sensation of someone watching her persisted. She turned slowly, but saw no one.

It was near the lunch hour, and the streets were crowded. Tourists, islanders, and business people crowded the sidewalks. She wasn't going to let her uneasy feelings spoil her day.

Adrienne loved this part of town with its twisted alleys and one-way streets. She sensed someone following her. She wandered in and out of the crowded tangle of people. She looked again, but saw nothing to cause concern.

In Angelique's Boutique, Adrienne talked with the owner, while keeping an eye on what was happening outside. She tried on several things and bought three outfits, including shoes and bags. She felt irresponsible for spending so much money on clothes. She hadn't done that in a long time, but she needed new clothes suited to the climate. She paid for her purchases and asked Angelique to deliver them to the cottage.

Leaving the shop, she glimpsed a man sitting at a table at the outdoor café across the alley. He was reading a paper. She had the feeling he was watching her.

She turned into Brick Alley. He wasn't far behind her. When she stopped, he stopped. When she moved on, so did he. So, she hadn't been wrong about being followed. He looked too well dressed to be a purse-snatcher. That she had seen him before niggled at the back of her mind. Brick Alley was strictly for pedestrians, always crowded, and she would be safe. Nervous, she still thought nothing could happen with all these people around.

Alex worried about her and would think nothing of having her followed. He would do something like that without her knowledge. She kept to the crowds and was relieved to see the end of the alley and the main road.

The man was still following her when she came to the intersection. Traffic moved along at a faster pace on the main thoroughfare. Standing in a group of people, she waited patiently for the walk sign to appear.

The light hadn't changed. The pressure of someone's hand on her back startled her. The forward push propelled her onto the cobblestone road. It sent her into the path of an oncoming car.

"Look out!" a man shouted.

Another man pulled her from the path of the car. He helped her up, but she passed out from sheer fright. When she revived, her head rested on someone's arms. She looked up into a familiar face.

"Steven?" she whispered.

"Hush now, my name is Tyler. Don't you remember? You were almost hit by a car. My name's Tyler Prescott."

Tyler's cane lay in the road a few feet away. The fuzziness in her head cleared, and it was Tyler holding her. Tyler saved her, not Steven. Why had she cried out Steven's name? Shaken, she wondered how she could have been mistaken.

A policeman hovered over them. "Mister Prescott, is the young lady alright?"

"Rudy, she's fine. Just a little shaken up."

"Miss Wyngate? I didn't know. I heard you were back. Should I call an ambulance for you?"

"I think I'm alright, except for some minor cuts," Adrienne replied. "My shirt's ripped, but otherwise I seem to be okay." Her voice was shaky. "Tomorrow I'll probably have a few bruises from hitting the pavement so hard, otherwise I'm fine. Tyler will take me to my own doctor."

It took Adrienne a few minutes to shake the feelings she had all day. She looked up at Tyler.

"What happened?"

"You tripped and fell in front of a speeding car. The driver didn't stop." He held her shaking hands and escorted her across the street to a sidewalk café.

The waiter approached at once. "What can I do for you, sir?"

"Brandy," Tyler ordered.

The waiter returned with a bottle and two brandy snifters.

What made Tyler think she had fallen? She grabbed the glass with both hands. She took a mouthful and swallowed. It burned going down. A boy retrieved Tyler's cane and was rewarded with a generous tip.

Adrienne didn't talk. Her suspicions that someone wanted to do more than hurt her had been confirmed. She put her glass down. Tyler took her hands in his.

"It wasn't an accident. I didn't fall. I was pushed," she whispered.

"Let's get out of here. You can tell me about it while I take you to your grandmother's."

"No, I'm alright, just a little shaken up. I'm supposed to meet her at Jolie's for lunch."

She was beginning to return to normal and thought about Tyler. What had he been doing in Old Town? She wouldn't mention she was being followed.

"I wasn't following you. The police asked me to come down and speak to them about Collette's disappearance. They thought I might have some information they could use."

"Did you?" She couldn't help but wonder.

"Only what everyone else knew. She worked for me for a few months until Friday when my manager fired her."

"Why did he fire her?"

"He caught her in my office going through some of my confidential documents. Files to which she had no rightful access."

"Were the papers important?"

"They were only to me. What time are you to meet Charlotte?"

"About one." She looked at her watch. "Oh, my gosh. I'd better get going."

"Where's your car?"

"I left it at Jolie's. It was such a nice day for a walk."

"I'll go back with you."

Tyler had a hard time getting up and leaned heavily on his cane. He had hurt himself saving her. It was something she wouldn't forget. He hailed a passing cab, and they rode the few blocks in silence.

When they reached the restaurant, she didn't ask him to come with her.

Adrienne couldn't let him leave after he rescued her. She reached over and kissed him on the cheek. She knew he wanted to return her affection, but felt him holding back. Was it because they were in a public cab? Maybe he thought better of it and changed his mind.

"When will I see you again?"

"Do you want to see me again?" Tyler's voice was polite.

"Yes, very much, I'm sorry I called you Steven."

"It's all right, Adrienne. A few years ago I lost someone I loved dearly. I wondered if I would ever get over it."

"The love I had for Steven will always be a part of me, but, it's time to store his memory away."

"Can you do it?"

"Yes, you showed me it can be done."

He took her in his arms and kissed her. It was a kiss filled with hunger and untold passion. A kiss that would hold them together for now and later when they were alone and could explore the feelings developing between them.

"Will you be at your grandmother's later today?"

"I'll be there or at the big house." Her grandmother would be upset when she found out about the accident.

"Good, because we have some matters to discuss."

They parted and she entered the restaurant, hoping she'd meet no one until she could clean up in the ladies room. However, Norman, standing at the bar, saw her enter.

"My God! What happened to you?" he said.

"I tripped and fell."

"It looks like it was more than just a fall."

"Damn it, don't be so observant," Adrienne growled.

"Sorry." His smile reached his eyes. "You have to know people and their reactions. Especially when it comes to talking and keeping your mouth shut. Come into my office where we can talk and try to make you presentable."

Once in the office, he went into the bathroom and came out with a clean facecloth, towels, and a first aid kit. He came to where she was sitting.

"Let me see that cut on your forehead?"

"I didn't know I had one."

"It's mean looking and has stopped bleeding. I'll clean it, put some salve and a Band-Aid over it." He worked methodically, cleaning and taping the gash on her forehead. "Wash your face and hands, and you'll almost look normal."

She came back from the bathroom and hugged Norman.

"Now that I've done my duty are you going to tell me what occurred?"

"Norman, I love you dearly, but I think its better that you don't know. I don't want anything happening to you or your family."

"Hey, that sounds awful."

"It's a lot of stuff I don't understand, and until I do, it's better for me to keep my thoughts to myself, so no one else gets hurt. What do you know about Tyler Prescott?"

"Just what Jolie told you. He has a good rep and is well liked. If you think he's behind this mystery of yours, I think you're barking up the wrong tree."

"Would you trust him with your life?"

"Alex doesn't trust anyone until he knows everything about them. They have been friends for some time. I'd trust him."

His words reassured Adrienne, and she reached over and kissed him.

"You'd better make an appearance or the ladies will wonder what happened to you," Norman said.

Chapter Twenty-Eight

A few days later, Tyler and Charlotte were already enjoying breakfast on the terrace of the beach cottage when Adrienne arrived. She sat down and joined them.

"You shouldn't be mad at Tyler for wanting to protect you," Charlotte said.

"I love you too much to let anything happen to you," he said.

Adrienne sputtered, her mouth full of coffee. She put the cup down and wiped her mouth with a napkin.

"You do?" Her smile brightened.

"Sometimes we're too protective of those we love." Tyler reached over to wipe a small piece of croissant from her chin.

She grabbed his hand as he was about to move it away. "Did you say you loved me?"

"Yes." He smiled. The words had slipped out. He had planned to wait until they were alone.

"How can you be sure you're in love with Adrienne?" Charlotte appeared astonished. "You've only known her for a few weeks."

"Sometimes a few weeks are enough," Adrienne said with a bright smile.

That she returned his love lightened Tyler's heart.

"I'm very happy for you," Charlotte said. "I'll leave you two alone. I have some calls to make. I'm sure you have a lot of things to discuss."

Tyler turned to Adrienne. "I surprised her. I think you knew how I felt."

"I've been expecting it." She grinned at him.

"Was I wrong in declaring my love in front of Charlotte?"

"No, she's part of my life, and what happens to me affects her too."

He rose and came around the table to lift her from her chair. The softness of her lips sent flames soaring through him. His tongue edged her lips apart, and he entered her mouth with searing passion. His body shuddered with pleasure. Her soft moans made him realize where they were, and he quickly released her.

"I love you, Adrienne, more than you'll ever know. This isn't the place or the time to show you how much."

"I love you, too. I agree there are too many things in our way. We'll have to sort them out."

"We will." This time he caught himself before using Steven's words of love.

"You needn't worry. Steven's love is just a memory. I can't live on memories. Memories are nice, but that's all they are. With you, there will be new memories, and the others will fade away."

"I know." How well he knew.

"I'd like to go up to the house and see what progress Hannah and George are making."

"It sounds like a good idea, but first I want to give you this." He removed a box from his jacket pocket and handed it to her. "I love you."

Surprised, she looked deep into his eyes. "Oh, Tyler, I love you with all my heart." She kissed his wanton lips and worked her way down to the opening of his shirt. It was a few minutes before they stopped.

He held her at arms length. "Adrienne, always remember, whatever happens, I love you."

* * * *

When Adrienne and Tyler arrived at the house, they found everything moving along expeditiously. George stood with his hands waving in the air, directing workmen in positioning the furniture. He finished his job before he noticed them.

George greeted her in his usual way by lifting her hand and kissing it. "Ah, my dear cousin, so you have decided to make an appearance." He still held her hand.

She smiled at him with a twinkle in her eye.

"We have a problem."

"What might it be?"

George had a tendency to magnify the smallest of details. "The trees are due tomorrow, and we have no idea where the Christmas decorations are."

"They're in the cellar behind the wines," Adrienne said. "Tyler, we'll need your help."

"Of course, anything I can do. I've been wanting to see those cellars."

She led them into the kitchen and through the pantry. A door on the far side opened to the stairs. She switched on a light, and they followed her down the stairs. She halted halfway down and looked around.

"Is there something wrong?" George said.

She turned and caught Tyler's eye warning her not to say anything. "I wasn't paying attention and stumbled. I guess I haven't outgrown my fears from years ago."

The men went forward. She bent down and picked up an earring that had caused her to stop. Collette wore one like it the night she dined with Tyler. What was it doing here?

Tyler watched George to see if he noticed the absence of spider webs or dust on the stairs, but he didn't and continued forward to the bottom. Adrienne caught up with them, unlocked the door, and turned on another light by the door. The door stuck. Warped with age, it wouldn't open.

"Damn, it's stuck," she said.

"Let me try it." It took all of George's strength and the help of Tyler to get it open. Inside, the room was cool. Row on row of dusty wine bottles lined the shelves.

"You had no lock on this door?" Tyler looked surprised.

"Never had any need. People who wanted our wine just had to come and ask. We had no thievery among our workers."

Tyler and George looked around.

"My God, have you any idea what these wines are worth?" Tyler said.

"Darling, I agree with Tyler," George added. "I'd advise you have this cellar inventoried and appraised as soon as possible, and put a good strong lock on the door. Things have changed."

"I'm tired of hearing those words. The island couldn't have changed that much. It'll have to wait until Monday when I return from Simone's."

"You're going to visit Simone?" Tyler looked unhappy.

"Yes, for the weekend. I've been promising her for some time."

They left the wine cellar and entered another room. George rushed to investigate the boxes marked Christmas lined against the wall.

"I don't like you driving that far alone," Tyler said to her.

"I promised Simone I'd come to see the ranch. She wants me to come this weekend." She stopped him before he could say anything. "I'm only going for the weekend and will be back late Sunday might."

"Those roads are lonely and dangerous as you already know."

"There's nothing to worry about. The other time was just some guy in a hurry."

"Call me as soon as you arrive and when you leave so Charlotte and I won't worry."

George, standing a few yards away looked at them, curiosity evident.

"Hey you two, hurry up. It's getting cold down here."

"What makes these so heavy?" Tyler said as he lifted a dust-coated box.

"The Carolers and the Crèche are made of solid wood. They're probably in that box."

"They've been around since I can remember," George remarked. "The Crèche makes a beautiful display when it's set up and has the right lighting."

"It sounds like it's beautiful to see," Tyler said as he turned to Adrienne. "Let's get out of here and leave this to George and his crew."

"Sounds like a good idea. It's all yours, George."

They left George exploring the boxes and returned upstairs. She told Hannah about the decorations and that George needed help. They said their goodbyes and left.

Walking, they took the beach way to Charlotte's and stopped to enjoy the afternoon sun and the soft breeze that wafted off the sea.

"Adrienne, have you any idea who might be behind your accidents?"

"I don't know why anyone would want to hurt me."

"You don't want to admit something is wrong or that one of your friends or relatives might be involved."

"Why should any of my relatives want to harm me? My father provided for them when he died. They were given ample funds for the rest of their lives."

"Maybe, for one of them it isn't enough," Tyler suggested.

"Do you have anyone in mind, or shall we go down the list of my so-called enemies? First, there's Simone. She's also my best friend. When she was younger, she was crazy about Peter. He treated her like a kid.

"My brother Elliot and Simone were engaged. She took his death hard. If he had lived, she would be mistress of Wyngate. She inherited her husband's ranch in the valley next to Peter's. Her husband left her very well off. The ranch makes a good income. She's shown little interest in the old mansion and seems quite content. I feel as though being away has left a chasm between us, and I don't want that. It's why I'm going out to the ranch for the weekend."

"How has she changed?" Tyler prompted.

"It's as though she's hiding something. I can't put my finger on it. Maybe she'll tell me when I see her."

"What about Peter?"

"Peter has been around as long as I can remember. We went out several times. There was no spark. Yet, for some reason people expected us to marry. He went to good schools. His family was well liked. He inherited the ranch and has run it for years. He's never married."

"You were about to be engaged to him when you met Steven."

"It was one of those things that old families take for granted. We were more like brother and sister than lovers. Luckily, I found Steven."

"Were there any hard feelings?"

"I think we were both relieved. We liked each other. I doubt our marriage would have lasted. Peter told me later I had made the right decision, and he liked being single."

"George has a playboy's reputation and is more fraud than the real thing," she continued. "He liked to shock people and make them sit up and take notice. He was always romancing the island's beauties and smart enough not to leave any children behind."

"What about the young lady working with him now?"

"I know nothing about her, but it looks like it might be the real thing. With George, one never knows. As for Jolie and Norman, I can count on their friendship at any time or hour. My father was the only one who believed in Jolie and lent her the money to start her business. She has money and Norman will inherit. She stayed friends with my parents until they died."

"Alex and his family have been on the island as long as ours. My sister Aimee was seventeen when they fell in love. The ten-year difference in their ages didn't seem to matter. He patiently waited until she turned twenty-one, and then they married. They were very much in love and only death came between them. I don't see how you could include Alex in your quest. He's supposed to be your friend."

"He is my friend. He isn't on my list of suspects."

"There's nothing for anyone to gain. I made arrangements the day I went to town and changed my will. There is nothing worth killing me for. There are a few bequests to my friends and the servants. No one would profit from my death, only the island Historical Society."

Chapter Twenty-Nine

The afternoon sun set as Adrienne drove the last few miles to the ranch. She had mixed emotions about going all this way for a weekend. Her feelings for Tyler and his warning to be careful lay heavily on her mind.

Driving automatically, Adrienne thought about other things. What was life without a husband and children? She knew how much she wanted a family. She and Steven had discussed it many times. She and Tyler hadn't had time to discuss it. She didn't want to burden her children with a three-hundred year-old Plantation home. She loved the place, and the plans she had made were right. Everything came down to Wyngate, her heritage, and her responsibility.

Adrienne had plenty of time to mull over the events since her arrival home. Even her grandmother was uneasy about the so-called accidents. It took a lot to rattle Charlotte. A few people had gone out of their way to warn her that the island had changed. Could it have changed that much in three years? She knew the answer. It had, and so had she.

The front gates to the entrance to the ranch stood wide open, and she drove down the three-mile road that would bring the hacienda into view. Freshly painted fences and barns greeted her. As she approached the hacienda, she saw brightly blooming flowers flowing from several window boxes to give the place a homey feeling. A small gate to the house was barred and locked. Two fierce mixed-breed dogs barked, as they raced back and forth along the fence.

A few minutes later, she saw Simone leave the house followed by a tall dark-haired ranch hand. He talked to the dogs, quieting them down. He didn't leave. Dark and virile, he was somebody she didn't know. She guessed him to be in his late thirties or early forties. With some men, it was hard to tell their age. He kept his eyes focused on Simone.

Simone unlocked the gate and motioned Adrienne to park her car in front of the house. Adrienne heard an exchange in Spanish she couldn't quite understand. Was the man warning Simone to be careful, or was there some other hidden meaning behind his words? He unhitched his horse from the railing post, climbed on, and nodded to Adrienne.

"Enjoy your stay, Miss Wyngate."

Before she could reply, Simone addressed her. "Adrienne, I'm so glad you could come."

Was Simone relieved the man had left or did she seem disappointed? She presumed the latter. Simone liked to have a bevy of beaus humming about her. Maybe this man was her lover.

"What are you thinking about?" Simone said, "You seem to be far away."

"It's been a long time since I was here. The place has changed. I'm realizing just how much we've grown up."

Her curiosity was getting the better of her. She wouldn't ask questions. Simone would tell her when she was ready.

"We updated the barns and intend to redo the house this fall. We do a little at a time. It takes money to keep this ranch going. Before dinner, we'll take a walk down to the barns to see the new Arabian colt. She's a beauty."

Adrienne hadn't missed the word 'we'. Who was she inferring? The ranch hand? "I thought you only raised cattle."

"We've gotten interested in Arabians. They're beautiful."

"That's an expensive hobby."

She wondered if her friend was as happy as she pretended. When the ranch hand came back, Simone introduced him.

"This is Chris, my foreman. Adrienne is the friend I've told you about."

"It's nice to meet you, Miss Wyngate."

Chris was polite when they shook hands. He acted little uneasy as though he wished to be somewhere else.

"He does everything on the ranch." Simone also seemed edgy.

Chris didn't act like the hired help. He seemed right at home in the house. If Simone wanted to have a lover, it was none of her business.

"Chris, please bring Adrienne's overnight bag in from the car."

"Okay," he replied.

The way he looked at Simone told Adrienne there was a lot more to their relationship. "Chris is new?"

"Yes, and he's a very good foreman."

Adrienne noticed Simone couldn't keep her eyes off the man. She didn't blame her. He was a hunk. He put her bag in the guest room and left.

"How are you making out with the heat?" Simone led her to the guest room.

"It's a lot easier now that I'm become acclimated." Adrienne dropped her purse on the bed and slipped off her jacket.

"I don't think I'd ever want to leave here," Simone declared.

"You're missing out on a lot. There's a whole different world out there. Someday I'll go back for a visit."

They left the house and started toward the barns a good distance away. Adrienne took in the scene before her. Fenced areas where cattle roamed and another field held horses. Brand-new fences separated the animals. Two new pickup trucks were parked by the barn.

Adrienne knew how much money it cost to keep a place this large from falling into disrepair. The insides of the barn were clean, and the animals looked fed and well cared for. They carefully approached the stall the colt was in. She had beautiful markings.

"Isn't she a beauty? Her name is Shalimar."

As they were about to leave, a phone rang at the other end of the barn. Chris, carrying a portable phone, hailed them. Simone went to reach for the phone, but he pulled back.

"It's for Miss Wyngate."

Adrienne was astonished that someone would be calling her here. "Who could it be?"

"Answer it and find out," Simone suggested.

A premonition of disaster overtook Adrienne as she reached for the instrument. The brisk and authoritative voice on the other end wasn't familiar.

"Miss Wyngate. My name is Horace Miler. I'm calling from Queen

Anne's Hospital. Your grandmother has had a heart attack. It's important you return right away."

Adrienne's heart sank. Tears rose in her eyes. "When did it happen," she managed to ask.

"It happened about half an hour ago."

"It'll take me a while to get there. I'm out in the valley."

"It's important you get here as soon as possible."

"I'm on my way." She didn't think to ask any questions. Stunned at the news, she automatically gave the phone back to Chris.

"Adrienne what's wrong?"

Simone's words finally penetrated Adrienne's brain. "I can't stay. My grandmother has had a heart attack and is in the hospital."

"Oh no, Do you want me to go with you?" Simone was sympathetic.

"There's no need. I'll call you when I know something."

Adrienne's heart pounded. She could feel herself sweating. They hurried back to the house in silence. She didn't see the look that passed between Simone and Chris. Adrienne retrieved her overnight bag and returned to her car. She gave Simone a hasty farewell kiss and returned her hug.

* * * *

Simone and Chris watched as Adrienne drove down to the main road. Chris put his arm around Simone. "It looks like we are going to have a busy night. Get your jacket and let's get moving."

Chris watched his wife go to the house. She was so sure, so wanton. He sighed, now wasn't the time to be thinking of those things. He took his phone and dialed a number he knew by heart. When someone answered, he spoke.

"Adrienne's on her way back."

"Follow her," the voice replied.

* * * *

Darkness descended as Adrienne left the ranch. She worried about Charlotte. She didn't dare speed on the narrow roads. Absorbed in keeping her mind on her driving, she didn't see a vehicle behind her until it was too late. The truck pushed her forward several times and then sideswiped her car.

Not again. She struggled with the wheel, trying to control the car. The truck came at her again, this time pushing her car into a rock and tree-shrouded ravine. She had enough sense to turn off the engine as the car rolled over and over to land upside down. In the gully, she felt like a rabbit being skinned and cut up for stew. Every part of her body hurt. In a semiconscious state, she heard voices shouting.

Chapter Thirty

Adrienne's head throbbed. Her insides churned like a cement mixer. Turning slightly, she opened her eyes to the darkness that surrounded her. When she woke, her pain shouted for relief. She looked around and wondered what she was doing in this strange bedroom? The room blazed with bright splashes of island color. She eased her way up to a sitting position.

Standing, Adrienne grew dizzy, and she had to wait a few minutes for it to cease. Still unsteady, she moved to the window. Below in the distance, she saw Wyngate Manor. She realized she was at Hunter's Lodge. What was she doing here?

She remembered the urgent telephone call telling her Charlotte had a heart attack. Was her grandmother all right? She left Simone's and drove the lonely road to town. The same brown truck that pushed her off the highway pursued her on the empty road. He kept it up until he pushed her car into a ravine. She remembered her screams of fright. Then…

* * * *

"It's alright. She had enough sense to turn the engine off and she was wearing her seat belt."

"Good! Let's get her out of there before the truck comes back. Whoever is paying him for his dirty work won't like it when he finds out he didn't finish the job. She looks pretty messed up. You know where you're to take her?"

Passing in and out of consciousness, the man's voice sounded familiar. She knew that voice. What was Chris doing here? He should be at the ranch with Simone.

145

She had to concentrate on finding out about Charlotte's condition.

* * * *

When she woke again, she was startled to see her robe at the foot of the bed. The nightgown she was wearing was one of her own. How did her clothes get here? Then she remembered her overnight bag. Someone must have retrieved it from her car.

The furnishings in the room were strange to her. She tried standing and grew dizzy. She sat down and slid her robe around her. Slowly, she got up again and managed to make her way to the French doors. An upstairs balcony lay beyond the doors. Standing outside, she let the rays of the sun warm her. Looking down over the hills, she saw Wyngate Manor standing majestically in the sunlight. This was Tyler's house. How did she get here? She needed a phone. There wasn't one in the bedroom. Her curiosity got the better of her, and she decided to explore.

Leaving the room, she entered a long hallway. To the left, she noticed a staircase leading down. She heard birds singing and fluttering about outside. They were the only sounds she heard.

Adrienne descended the stairs. Arriving on the lower floor, she gazed around. No one appeared to be about. She started to look into the rooms off the hall. One was a dining room and the next room was a library. The room she entered on the other side of the hall was an office.

She saw a phone on the desk. Several diplomas from engineering and architectural firms covered the walls. Tyler hadn't lied to her about his profession. She went to the desk to use the phone. With a sharp "whoop," she stopped.

A picture of her sat on the desk. The picture was one of a kind. She had it specially made and had given it to Steven. The inscription read. To Steven, with all my Love, Adrienne. What was it doing on Tyler's desk?

It came as a shock when she heard her words. "Tyler is Steven."

With tears in her eyes, Adrienne turned and blindly ran into Tyler standing by the door. He wore a robe over his swim trunks as he watched her. His hair was still damp. How long had he been standing there?

He came to her and put his arms around her. "Adrienne, don't be upset with me. I've waited so long."

Fierce anger flashed through her mind. "Who are you, and what do you want with me? If you're not Steven, who are you?

She was angry and didn't know what to believe. She shouted and tried slapping his face. It didn't do any good. He was much stronger and pulled her closer.

"Who are you? What are you doing with the picture I gave Steven?" she babbled on. "I only had one made, and it was for Steven alone." Adrienne was out of control and accused him of being a fraud.

"Shush, my love. I am Tyler Prescott and I'm Steven's cousin. Steven and I were brought up by our Uncle Charlie. Steven and I were often taken for brothers. Uncle Charlie was notified by the Sisters on Santa Clarita that Steven was badly injured. They tried to save his life, but there was little hope for him. Charlie flew him from the island to a hospital in Miami. He died there and is buried in the family plot next to his parents."

His robe came open and her hands felt the ridges on his scarred shoulders and back. The more she fought, the tighter he held her.

"Adrienne, stop hitting me."

"What do you want with me?" She was still upset.

Confused, she couldn't understand what he was telling her. He let her go and put his hand under her chin and lifted her teary face so their eyes could meet.

"The night you fell down the stairs at the Plantation House was no accident. I spoke those words of love to you. For you are my Cara Mia, forever. My love, forever."

"You knew it wasn't an accident."

"I knew." He tried to calm her.

"You believed me."

"I've believed everything you told me." He smiled at her.

"Cara Mia was Steven's name for me." She needed more convincing.

"The nuns found him on Santa Clarita. They did what they could for him before Charlie came." Slowly, he let her go.

"Steven left the club feeling nothing could stop the wedding. He was wrong. Three thugs jumped him after he left Peter and Alex. They beat the hell out of him and dumped him in the ocean. He came ashore on San Clarita Island."

"Our uncle, Charlie, was the gentleman who left you in the middle of the dance floor. He knew something was wrong. He knew I only loved you and wanted to marry you."

"Why would someone want to hurt Steven? He never hurt anyone."

"He was a threat to someone. I don't know why, only that those thugs left him to die."

"That's why he never turned up at our wedding. We didn't know what happened to him. I knew the note was false."

Tyler took her in his arms again and hugged her. "Coming here was the only way I could keep you safe. You have every right to be upset. Please, forgive me for deceiving you. It was the only way I could think to protect you. I fell in love with your picture. I knew I had to find out what went wrong. If you could understand the hell I went through. Wanting you, knowing I couldn't tell you the truth, because I was afraid for you."

"You're afraid for me, but why?"

"Steven's murder is linked to you."

"Everyone warned me about you, but I believed you weren't responsible for my accidents."

"Thanks for the vote of confidence," Tyler replied. "I'm afraid we got sidetracked. Your grandmother is quite well. The call was a hoax to get you back on the road so our perpetrator would have a clear shot at killing you."

He smiled down at her. "I had no choice but to suspect everyone connected to you."

"Is Wyngate Manor the main objective of our killer?" she said.

"I believe it is," Tyler replied.

"Who would want an old house?"

"It isn't so much the house as the land. It's a valuable piece of real estate. If you and Steven married and had children, he or she would inherit everything you have. His or her main objective is to keep you from marrying and having an heir to inherit."

On the spur of the moment, she smiled at him. "Tyler, will you marry me?"

"I'd be glad to, the sooner the better." He took her in his arms and kissed her.

"How about New Year's Day after the fireworks. We'll start the year right."

"It sounds wonderful to me."

"Who knows I'm here?"

"Everybody is here including your grandmother, Simone, Chris, and of course, my Uncle, Charlie."

"Why are Chris and Simone here?"

"They helped rescue you."

"Who is Chris?"

"I suppose after all these years you didn't recognize your Uncle Eric?"

She was stunned and surprised to learn Chris was Eric. "He can't be. He was killed many years ago."

"Chris is Eric with a new name so he could return home to discover who framed him. Simone recognized him and offered to help. He's been Simone's husband and foreman for two years. They're very much in love and wanted to keep it a secret. Eric offered their help when they learned you had returned to the island. We think the same person who wants to hurt you is the same person who tried to frame Eric on a charge of rape years ago."

"When can I see him?"

"Not for a while. They returned to the ranch. Don't tell anyone about Simone and Eric or what happened until we find out what's going on."

"Have you any idea whom it might be?"

"We think you stand in the way of his obtaining Wyngate Manor. We have detectives working to put the pieces together."

"The upkeep of Wyngate is horrendous. The only thing for someone to do is to get some financial backers to invest and turn it into a posh resort or tear it down. It will happen over my dead body." Adrienne told him.

"This person wants you dead."

"Who is it?"

"I'd rather not say until we're sure. So don't ask any more questions. The less you know, the better off you'll be."

"I'm to go about minding my own business while someone plans to kill me?"

"So far, we've been lucky. I think he's biding his time until the holiday celebration."

"That's just a few weeks away."

"Be patient, my love. Stay close to Charlotte, Alex, or me."

"It's nice to know the people I love the most aren't involved."

"What makes you think they aren't?"

"Don't do this to me. I have enough to worry about with the holidays just around the corner and Charlotte."

"Charlotte is quite safe. We're also watching over her. Just remember, I don't want you going any place alone."

"I have to check on the house arrangements to make sure everything is ready."

"Take Carmen with you."

"Why, Carmen?"

She's an expert shot and knows how to protect you. She's one of my people."

By the determined look on his face she could tell he wasn't going to relent and let her go alone, but she'd find a way.

"I've been watched ever since I returned home, either by you or one of your employees."

"It was the only way I could protect you."

Chapter Thirty-One

A faint glimmer of moonlight shone through the high windows of the Great Hall. Most of the pictures on the walls lay in darkness. The voices of other family descendants interrupted the silence. A person could hear them if they listened carefully. The voices of Sir John and the Contessa were missing. The paintings of them in the gold ornamental frames of the couple were lifeless.

"Where have they gone?" One of the more recently deceased spoke.

"He's taking her with him this time," another replied.

"They're traipsing around the house as if they owned it. You know how bored he gets hanging there."

"He generally goes alone," someone farther down the hall answered.

"It must be something important."

"Where do they get off being able to leave the hall?" the hundred-year-old newcomer complained.

"They're our forefathers, and rank has its privileges."

"Why don't you old fogies be quiet?" a buxom blonde hanging midway down the hall complained. "A person needs her beauty sleep? It's after midnight."

Many "harrumphs" were heard throughout the hall.

"The younger generation has no respect for their elders," Ashton Wyngate scolded.

"One has to be wise enough to know the history and undercurrents of the past to understand. Sir John and the Contessa often have the freedom to wander."

"They are the original owners of Wyngate," Abigail insisted.

The other portraits watched in silence as Sir John and the Contessa slid through the locked doors of the hall toward the main staircase.

* * * *

Johnnie and Theo stood arm in arm and looked down the winding stairs at what had once been their home.

"Oh, darling, can you believe it's almost Christmas?" Theo sighed as they glided down the stairs. "The white magnolias stand out magnificently against their waxy green leaves. The red ribbons draping over the banisters are just the way we did it."

"Yes, Theo, just like it was in our day. Adrienne has spared no expense. Can you imagine what the masked ball on New Year's Eve will be like? I can go around pinching all the young ladies bottoms, and no one will slap me. They'll have to blame their beaus or someone else. Oh, what fun it'll be," Sir John proclaimed.

At the bottom of the stairs, they moved into the hallway to view the huge Christmas tree. The wooden Crèche sat under the tree. Sir John bent down and lifted one of the figures to examine it.

"Oh, darling, they're as beautiful as when we bought them," Theo told him.

"I should hope so. They cost enough," Sir John replied with a crafty smile.

"I wonder if Adrienne knows what expensive heirlooms this house possesses."

"She knows the value of our treasures. I'm sure Charlotte has told her," Johnnie responded. "Our treasures have worth only to those who love them as much as we do. I'm quite sure Adrienne knows. Can you flip the switch darling? It should make the room glow."

"Is it this thing by the door?"

"Yes it is, my dear. We can only have it on for a few minutes. We don't want anyone to see the house lit up and come to investigate. You did put the sleeping potion in the guard's coffee?"

"Have I ever failed you when we have a mission in mind?" Theo replied.

"No, darling you haven't." Johnnie smiled at his lovely wife. "Flip the switch, and let's see what happens."

Theo flipped the switch and many glowing lights illuminated the hallway. The Christmas tree was decorated in fresh white magnolia blooms with their shiny green leaves, red velvet bows, and white candles.

Like a child on Christmas morning, the Contessa let out a cry of pure delight at the scene. She turned to Sir John. "Oh, Johnnie, it's magic."

"Come along, love. We have things to do." He took her hand, switched off the hall lights, and led her into the ballroom. He turned on the lights in the big room. The chandeliers sparkled like stars in the night sky.

"I'll say the moderns have come up with some jolly good ideas." Two large Christmas trees decorated with hand blown glass ornaments stood at each end of the ballroom.

"Adrienne is fortunate to have these new inventions. Our servants spent days cleaning and lighting the candles in the chandeliers. They had to use those noisy pulleys to lift the chandeliers and candles into place."

"What if someone sees the lights and comes?"

"The curtains are closed, and very little light can be seen, my Pussy Cat."

"Oh, Johnnie, you haven't called me Pussy Cat in centuries."

A harpsichord stood in a corner. Johnnie went over and turned the key. He lifted the top. The notes of the Blue Danube Waltz sounded through the room.

Johnnie took Theo in his arms, and they danced, softly humming along with the music only they could hear.

"What do you think of Adrienne's young man?" Johnnie said as he whirled Pussy Cat expertly around the dance floor.

"He reminds me of you in your younger days. When you were the dashing pirate and Sir John the aristocrat," she remarked.

After a moment, she spoke again. "I think the pirate. You were never a gentleman. Even now I can see the restlessness in you. You're up to something."

"How would you like to attend the New Year's Eve Ball?"

"Could we? I have nothing to wear, but this old dress."

"It's perfect for a costume ball. We'll come as ourselves and shock everyone."

"What fun it'll be. We haven't been to a party in decades."

"Centuries would be more like it, my dear," he teased as he pulled her closer.

"Won't Adrienne be upset?"

"Why should she be? We're family."

"How wonderful it'll be. We can eat and dance all night long. I always loved the fireworks. We'll watch them from the veranda and have a wonderful time." The Contessa giggled.

"It's a good thing we're able to come down off the wall once in awhile. Roaming through one's house isn't a privilege every ghost has. Some ghosts are so unhappy, they're confined to haunting."

"I know, my dear. We are the more fortunate ones, and we're not your average ghosts," Theo said in a superior manner.

"Wyngate Manor is our home, and we shall guard it forever."

"Adrienne is a Wyngate. She's the only one who understood our needs concerning the Manor and the treasures in it. She comes to us for advice when something bothers her."

"The other day, when Tyler was with Adrienne, we were talking about her ties to the past and what the house means to her."

The sound of men stumbling in the dark alerted them. They could see flashes of light.

"Theo, come and don't argue with me," Johnnie cautioned her in a warning voice she very seldom heard. "It's that evil creature again."

"Why must we always hide from him?"

"There's no time to explain. Come along, old girl, we have an advantage over the intruders."

Sir John turned off the lights and, taking the Countess's hand, slid out of the ballroom into the darkened hallway where they could observe the intruders. The gleam of a light showed briefly at Sir John as he bumped against a stand in the hallway. The light played its way up the staircase, stopping half way.

"Who's there?" a distorted voice they didn't recognize demanded.

When no response came to the question the culprit came halfway up the stairs. His light flashed in all the corners of the hallway.

"I don't see anyone here," one of the other intruders replied.

The man returned downstairs. He appeared suspicious. "Who's

there?" he demanded again. "If you don't come out, I'll shoot."

Again, no one answered. He turned his light toward the floor. A brown field mouse stood hypnotized in the light's beam.

"A damn mouse."

He raised his foot to crush it. He wasn't fast enough, and the mouse fled.

* * * *

His nerves were shot. He owed so much money to his supplier. He barely could afford to hire the thugs to do the job. This nonsense had to stop. After all, he belonged here. Why should he have to come stumbling around the house in the dark? The house rightfully belonged to him.

Tonight he needed some instant cash. It was the only place he could get it, pawning a few precious knickknacks Adrienne would never miss. She had lived in the lap of luxury for years. Now it was his turn. Soon the world would know the truth, and he would claim his rightful place.

"I am Master of Wyngate. This house rightfully belongs to me," he shouted and then laughed.

* * * *

At first the ghosts heard his laugh as soft and gentle. Then it grew into the hysterical laughter of an obsessed maniac. The loud sound echoed through the open halls, rattling the timbers of the old house. Sir John and Theo grimaced at the horrible laughter.

"The Devil is here again," Johnnie whispered to Theo. "He never will be master of Wyngate. We must do something."

The three men sprayed paint over the furniture and pulled the Christmas trees apart. Ornaments shattered when they hit the floor.

"This has got to stop," Johnnie said to Theo.

"I'll take care of those two," Theo replied. "You take care of the Devil."

She gracefully slithered across the room and tapped one man on the shoulder. When he turned, she tapped the other man on his shoulder. This went on for a few minutes. Theo watched in amusement as they turned to each other and started throwing punches.

"Joey, why did you hit me?"

"I didn't hit you."

Joey jumped as a hand pinched his buttocks. Manny felt a fist hit him in the jaw.

"Why did you do that?"

"I didn't hit you. Keep your hands to yourself."

"What do you mean?"

The Devil's voice entered the fray. "What the hell are you two doing? I'm paying you good money to do this job. Not to argue between yourselves. Get back to work."

The men were angry.

Before the Devil could leave, he heard a woman's voice coo to him as she wrapped her arms around him and kissed him.

"Do you like that, my friend?" The words were soft and caressing.

Another voice reached his ears. "You will never become master of Wyngate."

The Devil shook himself and, like the other two men, ran for the quickest way out. He kept repeating there were no such things as ghosts. He ran scared and shaking to his old brown truck.

Theo took Johnnie's arm and surveyed the room. "Look at the mess they made. We won't be able to have a ball." Tears appeared in her eyes. Johnnie took her in his arms.

"I'm sure Adrienne will make it happen." He pulled her closer and held her until her tears stopped.

They glided up the staircase, down the hall, and through the great doors to their resting place. As they settled back in their frames, Sir John spoke to his ghostly companions.

"There's a madman who thinks he can lay claim to Wyngate. We all know it's impossible. The Masters of Wyngate may have been eccentric and a little weird at times, but there has never been a madman in charge. It'll only happen over my dead body."

Snickers could be heard by the other family members.

Theo, with her ever-knowing smile, spoke to her husband. "But darling, you are dead."

Chapter Thirty-Two

It was a week before Christmas. The master bedroom at Hunter's Lodge resembled a lover's boudoir after a long night of passionate and satisfactory lovemaking. Adrienne lay sprawled over Tyler's body exploring two jagged scars covered by curly black hair.

"What's so compelling about my body?"

"Everything," she said as she curled into him.

He pulled her tighter into his arms. "You're definitely a descendant of those ancestors hanging on the walls in the Great Hall. At times you're quiet and very sedate, and other times a hellion. Last night you were like a female tiger having her first good meal in some time."

"Can you blame me?"

"How I've waited and prayed for this day to come."

He resumed kissing her and soft sighs of pleasure escaped her. He was slowly working his way down to her breasts when the telephone rang. "Who the hell can be calling at this hour?"

"You might try answering it." Adrienne admired her engagement ring.

An ominous feeling of disaster came over her as the ringing continued its urgent cry. It was seven o'clock in the morning. They didn't have to be at her grandmothers until ten.

"This is Chief Inspector Gregory calling. Mister Prescott, is Miss Wyngate with you?"

"Yes, she is Chief inspector. Just one moment and I'll put her on."

Adrienne didn't like what she saw in Tyler's expression as he handed her the phone.

"It's Chief Inspector Gregory," Tyler told her.

"Yes, Chief Inspector, this is Adrienne Wyngate. Is something wrong?"

"There has been a break-in at Wyngate. I think you should come as soon as possible."

"A break-in? The alarm system is on all the time. How bad is it?"

"I think you should see for yourself."

"Thank you. Tyler and I will be there shortly."

She stared at Tyler. "There's been a break-in at the house." Tyler took her in his arms to calm her.

"Let's get dressed and we'll see," he said.

"I need to shower first." She pulled away.

"Alright, Carmen will have coffee ready."

Adrienne puzzled over the possibilities as she headed for the shower. Too many unknown factors were entering her life. She had to learn who wanted Wyngate badly enough to kill for it.

* * * *

Three police cars were parked in the front driveway when Adrienne and Tyler arrived. A policewoman, guarding the door, greeted them.

"Miss Wyngate, Mister Prescott, the Chief is expecting you. Go right in."

"Thank you." Adrienne entered the foyer and gasped in dismay. The amount of damage shocked her.

"What have they done to my beautiful home?" she cried.

Tyler held her hand more tightly and pulled her closer. "Just remember, I'm with you. Everything will be alright."

"I'm afraid it looks worse than it is," the Inspector informed her. He was a tall thin man, with a graying moustache, wearing smartly tailored khaki shorts and a short-sleeved shirt. "Miss Wyngate. I'm Chief Inspector Gregory. I'm sorry we have to meet this way."

He gave Adrienne a smile that said he liked what he saw. The perusal was done in the blink of an eye. She wouldn't have noticed it unless she was looking directly at him.

"It's nice to see you again, Prescott." Obviously the two men had met before. "Before we go any farther, I think you should know the vandalism was done methodically."

She saw several pieces of furniture in the hall were scarred with a knife or some other kind of sharp instrument. The upholstery on several chairs in the ballroom had been cut, and the stuffing pulled out. Paint spattered the walls, and several pictures were now just globs of color. Her heart sank. What would Charlotte do when she saw the mess? She didn't have to wait long.

Charlotte entered the house like a cyclone. A policeman came with her.

"My God, what kind of a maniac would ruin precious paintings and antiques like these?" Her hand swept through the air, including everything she could see.

The magnolias had been pulled off the Christmas trees. What was left was painted a ghastly orange and purple. The nativity scene lay in a jumble on the floor. The heavy pieces had been thrown against the wall and left where they fell. Absently, Adrienne reached down and picked up one of the lambs and fondled it. Tyler took her hand and the lamb in his.

"The detectives want everything left as it is. They still have a lot of pictures to take for evidence," A young police officer informed them.

Instead of letting the lamb go. Adrienne held onto it for support and strength. She had no idea why she needed the lamb. Something to reassure her that things would be all right now that she had Tyler by her side. He loved her.

Who hated her enough to want to ruin an old relic like Wyngate? She looked at her grandmother daintily wiping away tears. She was trying not to shed them. Adrienne knelt by Charlotte and slipped the wooden animal into her hands. There were several sheep in the display and one less wouldn't matter. The animal's coating had split.

"It'll be alright, everything is insured and what isn't, can be replaced." Adrienne told her grandmother.

"Some of these things have been passed down from our forefathers and are irreplaceable. They mean so much."

"The vandals were evidently scared off in their attempts to steal more expensive items," the Chief Inspector told them. "We found a bag of antiques and some spray cans in the kitchen plus some burglary tools scattered about. They seem to have left in a hurry. Whatever scared them must have been big to make them take off without their loot and tools."

"You're new on the island?" Adrienne said.

"About six-months," he responded.

"I've been back just a few weeks." There was a slight smile on her face "You have probably heard the rumors about the ghosts of Wyngate."

"I've heard rumors to that effect. Do you believe ghosts haunt your house, Miss Wyngate?"

"Of course, Chief Inspector. I wouldn't be a Wyngate if I didn't. Do you believe in ghosts?"

"There are many things in life that can't be explained. I've been trained to expect the unexpected. Evidence is an important part of what I do."

"I understand."

She wondered if Sir John was listening to their conversation. She wouldn't put it past the old rascal. Was he the one who scared the thieves away?

The Chief Inspector was watching her. She gave him an angelic smile.

"Sergeant Higgins. Please take Miss Wyngate and Mr. Prescott through the house to see if anything else is missing. I want to check on the photographer and the print man to see if they've come up with any clues." The Inspector turned to the waiting police officer.

"Higgins will go with you. He's a very thorough man and knows his job."

"I'll stay here. I don't feel up to seeing the massacre," Charlotte told them.

"I think it's a good idea, Charlotte. Is there anything you need before we go?" Tyler leaned toward her.

"No thank you, Tyler. If I need anything, I'm sure one of those nice policemen will get it for me."

Higgins led them into the ballroom. The Christmas trees lay on the floor with their smashed ornaments sparkling in the sunlight. Some ornaments hung precariously on the trees, as though the vandals just grabbed what they could reach. Colored glass was scattered over the floor. Luckily, the harpsichord seemed to have missed the carnage.

The overhead chandeliers remained intact, most likely because it took three or four men to raise and lower them. She could imagine what the ballroom would have looked like if they had fallen. Waterford crystal ornaments were smashed to smithereens. It would take weeks to clean up the mess. Chairs and tables lining the ballroom were ripped and spattered with paint. This time it was an abhorrent yellow.

"Is there anything missing?"

"We never keep much furniture in here. The rest of the table and chairs only come out when we are having an affair. We left a few tables and chairs throughout the room. So it wouldn't look so bare."

In the library, books were taken from the shelves and thrown on the floor. Ancient volumes, pages ripped and their backs broken, looked forlorn. Again it was the same story only up to a certain level of the shelves. The thugs who did this hadn't tried to reach higher.

"There were a set of cloisonné vases and several ivory figurines my grandfather had brought back from China."

"I believe those are the things we found in the kitchen," Higgins said. "Is there anything else, Miss?"

"There are several small pieces missing." They went from room to room and found the same odd scenario in them. Nothing was touched above a certain height.

Tyler who had been quiet, had apparently noticed that too. "Guess they weren't especially tall."

"It looks like they couldn't reach any higher and were running out of time. The farther back they went in the house, the less damage they caused."

"They grabbed what was in reaching distance. It didn't seem to matter if the items were worth any money or not." Tyler observed.

"There had to be more than one man. Something scared the hell out of them to make them leave all their stash by the back door," Higgins suggested.

Behind Higgins's back, Tyler tried not to smile at the mischievous look in Adrienne's eyes. They both knew who had scared the vandals.

"Shall we go upstairs?" Higgins said.

"Yes, let's go." Adrienne was curious.

She wanted to visit the Great Hall and talk to Sir John. She knew it was impossible with Higgins's trailing along. She led the way with Tyler by her side.

"We've been lucky so far. The night watchman was only tied up and drugged."

"If he has any injuries, have the hospital send the bill to me."

"Yes, Miss Wyngate."

Adrienne felt better, knowing that whoever did this hadn't seriously hurt anyone. Checking out the upstairs bedrooms, they found them to be free of vandalism. Some knickknacks were missing. At that moment, another policeman came looking for Higgins.

"The Chief wants you downstairs."

"Tell him I will be right there. I sure would love to see the rest of the house, but duty calls."

"We will make it another time, Sergeant," Tyler told him.

"I'll have to bring my wife on one of the tours."

"Tell you what, Sergeant, after the New Year, Miss Wyngate will be glad to give you and your wife a personal tour." Tyler took a card out of his pocket and handed it to the policeman. "Call me at this number, and we'll make the arrangements."

"Thank you, sir. Good day to you, Miss." Higgins departed.

They watched Higgins walk down the corridor to the main staircase.

Tyler turned to Adrienne. "I hope you don't mind my suggesting it."

"No. Why should I? He looks like a nice young man."

"I'm glad. I couldn't stand the way he kept looking at you with those puppy brown eyes."

"Are you jealous?"

"Very much so. I have no intentions of sharing you with anyone."

"And I have no intentions of sharing you either."

"Let's go visit those impossible, mischievous relatives of yours to find out what happened last night."

Adrienne turned on the lights in the Great Hall. The sounds of snoring and little snuffs and snorts came from numerous members of her family. Johnnie and Theo were still sleeping or they were playing possum.

Adrienne went ahead and softly tapped on the frame housing Sir John's portrait. He slowly opened one eye and looked down at her.

"My dear girl, what are you doing up at this ghastly hour?"

"It's eleven-thirty in the morning." Adrienne had looked at her watch.

Theo opened her eyes, startled, and then looked down at Adrienne. "You keep ungodly hours, young lady. What's the matter? Why are you waking us so early?"

"There was some excitement in the house last night."

"Excitement?" Sir John acted the innocent.

"What kind of excitement?" Theo prompted.

"You know what I'm talking about. You scared the vandals away." Adrienne couldn't help smiling.

"Are you accusing us of causing mischief?" Johnnie tried to scowl. It didn't work.

"Would I accuse my ancestors of haunting these elegant halls?"

"Adrienne dear, you should have seen your great-grandfather. He was at his very best, chasing those ruffians out the door," Theo exclaimed.

"Hush, dear. We had to do something. They were making enough noise to wake the dead. No pun intended. This motley crew of Wyngates cringed behind their frames. A fine lot of house haunters they turned out to be. We did it by ourselves. It was quite frightening at first, but we had a great time scaring the pants off them. We haven't had such a good time in centuries." Johnnie turned to Theo. "We must do it again, my dear."

"You scared the intruders away," Adrienne confirmed.

"Good. Maybe he'll stop roaming the house and leave us in peace."

"Someone has been visiting the house at night?" Adrienne looked from one to the other.

"Oh, yes. Didn't you know?"

"No, I didn't. Do you have any idea who it might be?"

"We never see his face. He hides behind a mask and slinks around like a snake. It was him and his gang. He'll think twice before coming back here."

"You won't be able to have the New Year's Ball," Johnnie said, clearly disappointed.

Adrienne went up to the painting and stroked her hand along his cheek.

"You needn't worry. There'll be a ball. Just like old times,"

Adrienne reassured them.

Johnnie perked up. "Did you hear that, my descendants? We are going to have a ball."

Whispering could be heard all through the hall.

"We will do what we can to fix things up between now and New Year's," she said.

When Tyler and Adrienne left the hall, she turned back and saw Johnnie winking at her. She wondered what he was planning. She knew better than to go back and ask. She would just have to wait and see.

Chapter Thirty-Three

The days between Christmas and New Years passed in a blur. George, Hannah, and the decorating/cleaning crews worked their magic. They repaired what could be fixed in time for the affair.

Adrienne spent long hours with the staff, answering phone calls and queries about the ball. The staff made sure all the arrangements for the ball went smoothly.

* * * *

The chandeliers glowed and candles in glass chimneys lit the rest of the house. They gave Wyngate Manor a feeling of warmth and happiness.

Guests arrived in every mode of transportation. From boats moored in the bay to horseback and carriages, adding flavor to the reality of the occasion.

The butler announced the guests as they arrived. They were greeted by the matriarchs of Wyngate, Charlotte, and her granddaughter, Adrienne. Compliments flew back and forth. The murmur of jubilant laughter and conversations were heard throughout the rooms.

"It's delightful to be here again," a smiling woman said excitedly. "My family never missed a ball. It was always so beautiful."

"Thank you," Charlotte replied. She received the Island's traditional greeting, by being kissed on both cheeks.

"Adrienne, dear, it is so nice to see you again. The decorations are magnificent," another couple declared.

Adrienne watched Tyler enter the room dressed as a riverboat gambler. He stood back and leaned on his cane. Tyler had been overdoing it and his leg had been fine, until this afternoon. She hoped it wouldn't keep him from joining her in a few dances.

Everything was set in motion. The Chief Inspector had a theory and, if he was right, the assailant would strike tonight. The last guests to arrive had been announced. Adrienne approached Tyler so he could escort her into the ballroom. They heard a commotion behind them and turned to see its cause.

Gasps of surprise came from Adrienne and her guests. Johnnie and Theo were descending the stairs, arm in arm. Startled by the appearance of her ancestors, she grabbed Tyler's arm for balance. Theo and Johnnie stood at the bottom of the stairs accepting well wishes and compliments from the other guests. Many of the ladies squealed in delight at the newcomers. The oohs and ahs were meant for the two beautiful people amusing her guests.

Adrienne held her breath and kept smiling as the butler unperturbed announced them. "Ladies and Gentlemen, may I present, Sir John Wyngate and his lovely wife, the Contessa Theodora."

Tyler stepped forward and greeted the couple. "It is our honor to have your presence at this gala affair."

He acted as though their appearance was nothing unusual. He kissed Theo on both cheeks and shook hands with Sir John.

Adrienne, overtaken by astonishment, tried not to let it show. She heard Tyler's words and moved forward to greet her guests.

Under her breath, Adrienne whispered to Sir John. "What are you up to?"

Sir John winked and smiled. "We've come to dance and party."

They entered the ballroom in their painted finery and before she moved to follow another guest stopped her.

"Adrienne. How imaginative. You hired actors to pose as your ancestors."

"Dear, the whole island will be talking," another woman chimed.

"It is absolutely fantastic, my dear girl," the woman said with a jealous glint in her eyes.

Adrienne and Tyler couldn't move onto the dance floor without someone stopping them to pay a compliment.

Tyler pulled her closer and whispered in her ear. "You didn't say anything about hiring actors."

"I didn't. They really are Sir John and Theo." She gave him an angelic smile.

She thought Tyler was going to choke. She was amused at the shocked look on his face.

"They needed to get away from their stuffy surroundings for a bit." She smiled at him.

Sir John tapped Tyler on his shoulder. "Hope you don't mind, young man. It's not often I get to dance with so many pretty young ladies."

Looking toward Theo and her partner, he nudged Tyler. "It looks like Theo needs to be rescued."

Tyler had his orders. He wasn't happy about Adrienne being with someone else, not even her ghostly ancestor.

He watched as Sir John gallantly swept Adrienne into his arms and into the dance. Tyler did as he was told and rescued Theo from some clown stepping all over her feet. She moved out of the other man's arms into his. Tyler smiled at her.

"Are you having a good time, darling?" Theo smiled as she moved closer to him.

"Of course, it's not often I have the honor of dancing with a beautiful ghost."

"Thank you, darling. Now that you're going to be part of the family, we'll have to do this more often," she said.

"I'm looking forward to it."

She was light as a feather. He swung her around the dance floor to a waltz. Before she could say anything more, Sir John and Adrienne moved closer.

Johnnie whispered to Theo. "You look magnificent, my dear."

At Johnnie's remark, Theo looked at him with one arched eyebrow. "Have you been raiding the wine cellar again?"

"I promised you I would be on my best behavior tonight. I haven't been imbibing in the wine. I only pinched a few young ladies."

Adrienne couldn't suppress her smile.

"You would have thought us mad, our wanting to come to your party. Don't you think our entrance added a dash of sparkle to the gala? It will be talked about for years to come." Theo giggled.

"As if the Wyngates aren't talked about enough. You know ghosts don't photograph. How do you think our guests will react, when they see the photos they have taken showing them on the dance floor alone?"

"They saw us with their own eyes, darling. It will make believers out of them," Theo said.

"Or scare them to death to find me dancing with my future wife's great-grandmother who has been dead for a few hundred years," Tyler added.

"Adrienne, aren't you enjoying yourself?" Sir John said.

"I'm enjoying myself too much."

"Stop worrying. No one knows the truth."

"Theo and you made a grand entrance," Adrienne reminded him.

"Of course, we always do. A masquerade ball is all about intrigue and surprise. You have the opportunity to deceive your friends and enemies. By the way, your enemy is here. I can feel him."

"You said enemy. There is only one?"

He ignored her question. "He's been roaming the house off and on for months, as though he owned it."

"He wants the house?"

"We won't let him have it," Johnnie replied.

"It's a man? How do you propose to stop him? You said you and Theo were the only ones who scared the intruders away. What were my father and brother doing?"

"They haven't been dead long enough to leave the hall."

"How long does a body have to be dead to leave the hall?"

Again, he ignored her question. "That's quite a nice ring your young man gave you."

"I'm glad you like it. Charlotte is going to announce our engagement at breakfast. Yes, he told me, he was Steven's cousin. You knew who he was when I introduced him to you and Theo."

"Would it upset you if we ever lost our lovely home?"

"Of course it would. Why would I lose Wyngate? It will live forever." Adrienne was shocked at his question.

"Don't be too sure, my dear. Life doesn't go on forever." Johnnie was in a melancholy mood.

"It has for you and Theo." She smiled at him.

"This will end too, my dear. Change is inevitable, whether we like it or not. You've taken good care of us."

Johnnie left off abruptly and started with a new thought. "Theo and I won't be staying long. We tire very easily these days. She wanted to come so badly. You know I can't refuse her anything." He left his thoughts unfinished. "Never mind it isn't important. As long as you are taking care of us nothing else matters. Were you upset at us coming?"

"Why should I be? You've livened up the party."

Johnnie looked tired.

"This party will be the talk of the island for years to come," someone said.

"I'm sure it will be. My love, all I can tell you is to be careful. Your enemy doesn't give up easily. Be very cautious and know that we love you."

"I will. There are several people watching over me."

Sir John bowed, lifted her hand, and kissed it. He then melted into the crowd.

Later, she saw him dancing with several of the guests. After awhile, Johnnie and Theo appeared together at the ballroom doors.

"Good evening everyone, and thank you all for a lovely evening." They gracefully ascended the spiral staircase and disappeared into the darkness.

Adrienne had been entertaining her other guests and had little time to chat with Simone and Chris. She saw Simone dancing with Peter. She didn't look happy. Adrienne was excited to learn her uncle was alive and living on the ranch with Simone. Her Uncle Eric cut in on Peter and Simone who gave him a most bewitching smile. Peter looked annoyed and went after one of the Altman sisters.

Jolie and Mister Farnsworth sat in a group with other guests talking to her grandmother. Norman was dancing with his wife as George was with his pretty associate. Off in a corner, Alex and Tyler were carrying on a lively conversation. Their eyes watched her.

Adrienne was in her own home with her family and friends gathered around her. Yet one of them wanted her dead.

Out in the bay, the fireworks lit the sky in bursts of color. Her guests moved out to the terrace to view the sparkling display. She'd been warned by the Chief Inspector to stay close to Tyler and Alex.

Chapter Thirty-Four

It was early morning, New Year's Day. The fireworks were over, and the guests were leaving. A few of the family's closest friends were invited to share an early morning breakfast.

Adrienne approached the dining room doors and was surprised to hear loud voices. She entered to see who was shouting and found Simone arguing with Peter.

"Peter, we know you own the brown truck that caused Adrienne's accidents," Simone said.

"How can you make a statement like that? I love Adrienne."

"You have never loved anyone but yourself. You don't know what the word means," Simone shouted angrily.

"How dare you insult me?" he shouted back.

"Your truck had damage that matches the paint from Adrienne's car."

Adrienne listened as Simone continued to accuse Peter of being the owner of the truck that twice ran her off the road. Peter was furious. His denials, despite his loudness, were unconvincing.

She started backing from the room, when Peter's harsh voice stopped her.

"Come in, Adrienne. Join the party." Quickly, he went over and pulled her roughly into the room, locking the door behind them.

Adrienne was stunned. "What are you doing with a key to the dining room?"

Peter's face was a mask of hate and ugliness. "I stole them, just like everything else in Wyngate that belongs to me."

She was learning some heartbreaking revelations about her

childhood friend. "Nothing here belongs to you."

His arrogance shocked her as did the accusations he was making. Before he could reply, she heard a sob from Simone.

"Stop your sniffling, you meddling idiot."

Adrienne saw fright in Simone's eyes. She didn't have to guess what was going on. Peter was drunk. He raised a hand to hit Simone. She ducked the blow and backed away.

Adrienne had never seen Peter so brutal before. He had always been kind and understanding when tragedy hit her family. He wasn't acting like the man she knew and had considered marrying before she met Steven. He stood looking at her with hatred in his glazed eyes.

The enemy had come forward. The man who once professed to love her and her family stood in front of her behaving like a raving maniac. The only emotion she could feel for him was fury for having been taken in by such an egotistical jackass.

Simone sought refuge behind one of the large chairs at the end of the dining room table. Her face was now one of rage. "He wants to kill you and claim Wyngate as his own," Simone sobbed. "Don't believe anything he says. He's stoned and drunk."

Simone was upset and frightened as Peter stood swaying back and forth, sneering at them. He ignored Simone's sniffling and turned to Adrienne.

"You should have married me. I was so close to being Master of Wyngate until Steven came along and stole you from me. Now there's this man Prescott."

"Steven didn't steal me from you, and neither did Tyler. We had agreed that if we met someone else, we would part as friends. There would be no hard feelings. We were friends, nothing more. I told you several times I wasn't in love with you."

"You loved me," Peter whined.

"I loved you like a sister loves her brother, and I considered you a good friend."

Adrienne wasn't afraid. She believed Peter to be sick. Where was Tyler? What was keeping him so long? Peter was in a trance.

From a hidden passage, Eric watched his enemy, waiting for a chance to attack. Peter was weaving back and forth as he rambled.

"If Sir John hadn't stolen Theodora and my grandfather's gold, I would own all this. Not you, you bitch."

Adrienne froze in horror. Peter's words were becoming nastier. She heard noises outside the door. She moved away from his hurting words. What had happened to the man who was once Peter Llewellyn?

"If you had married me, I wouldn't have had to steal to get what was rightfully mine. I've hated you and your family ever since I learned who I really was. You had everything that belonged to me. The only way I could get it was by marrying you. After a few years, you would get sick and die just like Monica. She had already signed everything over to me. She wanted a divorce when she learned my dirty little secrets."

"You murdered your wife, Monica?"

"Don't look so surprised. She was a liability. It was necessary. If I hadn't, she would have gone on telling everyone lies about me. I couldn't afford to have people know my secrets."

He brought the open bottle from the table up to his mouth, taking a long drink, but keeping his eyes on them. Then he put the bottle down. He became very talkative and disoriented.

"What secrets are you talking about?" There was more banging on the doors.

"Yes, both women are in here," Peter shouted. He looked at Simone as she tried to appease him.

"Peter, we love you. Please stop this nonsense." She moved toward him and stopped. The gun he held was pointed at her. "Shut up, you slut. I know about you shacking up with that lowly drifter."

"That lowly drifter, as you call him, is Eric Wyngate," Simone snapped.

"It can't be him. He's dead."

"No he's not," Simone shouted.

Peter looked from one to the other in astonishment. "Eric is dead. I had him killed. He's dead, just like Steven."

"I am afraid not, Peter."

Stunned, Peter turned and saw a tall man dressed as a Caballero, entering from a panel hiding a secret passage.

"You should hire men who do the job right. Lucky for me, you didn't check on them. Put the gun away, Peter," Eric demanded. "It'll settle nothing. Let's talk."

He moved closer, constantly keeping his eyes on Peter's movements. Again, Peter waved the gun back and forth between them.

Adrienne waited for the right moment, watching her uncle closely for the moment when Peter made a mistake. Whatever drug he was using made him talkative. She hoped Eric would keep him talking so she could gauge her attack.

"He's crazy," Simone cried out.

Her words infuriated Peter.

"Are you crazy, Peter?" Adrienne moved closer. "When you desire something too much, it has a tendency to make you a little crazy." She paused. "You want Wyngate Manor?"

"Yes, I want Wyngate, the 'Dead Man's Gold,' and all that goes with it." The sinister smile never left his face.

"You're not happy with what you have?"

"I have a ranch with three-thousand acres, and it's mortgaged to the hilt. It isn't worth a damn. Working my butt off day and night, to make ends meets is what I have. That's for the peasants. I'm no peasant. I'm a Llewellyn. I deserve to be treated like a gentleman and given respect."

Adrienne didn't know what respect he was talking about. "You're already a highly respected rancher."

She had to keep him talking. "How many of my family did you kill?" Adrienne struggled to keep the tears from flowing.

"I killed anyone who got in my way, including Steven. If you married him, you would have children. I couldn't let it happen."

"My mother, my stepmother, my brother, and Steven," Adrienne turned pale and rested her hands on the back of a dining chair for support, so she wouldn't falter.

As Peter continued his tirade, gloating, he emitted an ugly laugh.

"But why?" His viciousness stunned her.

"Why not," he replied sarcastically. "If you had accepted my proposal of marriage, none of this would have happened."

"It didn't work out the way you planned." Adrienne tried to keep her voice steady.

"No, your father had to come back from Europe married to Francine. Like all women, she became too demanding. She was another obstacle in my way. I had to get rid of her, like Collette.

"You killed Collette?"

"You needn't worry. Your brother's not alone. Your stepmother and Collette are keeping him company." Peter snickered.

"Where?" she demanded. With his revelation, she thought she might take a knife off the table to kill Peter herself.

Eric moved closer. "Adrienne, don't do any thing foolish. He's sick and will do anything to gain what he believes is his."

"Heed his warning, my love."

"I'm not your love and never was."

"You'll always be my love. Now if I told you where the bodies were hidden, it wouldn't be a secret any more. You'd want to go off to find them, and I don't have time for such nonsense."

"You call killing several people nonsense because they got in the way of your greed and your obsession."

Peter talked of his murders as if they were an everyday occurrence. She watched Simone edge closer to the table. Once, Adrienne had thought of marrying Peter. Thank God Steven came along when he did.

"As for sweet Aimee, I couldn't let her have an heir. All would be lost. Killing became my passion. A passion no woman could match. I couldn't quench my thirst for blood. It was so easy after the first one."

Peter was lost in his own world, giving Adrienne a chance to act. He finally looked up when he heard the pounding on the doors. He didn't see Adrienne pick up the heavy ornate silver candelabra from the table and throw it, hitting him in the face. He screamed as he tried to brush off the hot wax. One candle fell on the tablecloth setting it on fire. The other candle dropped from his face and landed near the curtains, which burst into flames that shot their way up the walls. The dining room rapidly filled with smoke.

The dining room doors flew open. In rushed Tyler and Alex. The men, including Eric, tried to lift Peter off the floor as he screamed for help. Peter's face and hands looked badly burned. Adrienne knelt down and took his head in her lap.

Tyler bent down next to him. "Where are the bodies?"

The flames rapidly engulfed the room. There wasn't much time to question Peter. His maniacal laugh sent shudders through Adrienne.

174

Peter's voice faltered as he tried to speak. "It doesn't matter anymore. They're in the lowest cellar." Angrily, he pulled away and rolled on the floor.

"Oh, Peter. All this killing for an old house. It wasn't worth your life."

He didn't hear her last words. He was dead.

Tyler pulled Adrienne away from Peter's body and brought her into his arms. The tears came in full force. Tyler led her from the flaming room.

"Everyone heard him tell you he killed your family. He has paid for his sins."

They were lucky to escape the burning room. They soon realized the flames were spreading to other parts of the house. Too soon, a roaring conflagration was consuming everything.

Adrienne grabbed Tyler's arm. "We need to save Sir John and Theo." Adrienne raced up the staircase to the Great Hall.

Tyler followed. "Stop! Come back. This is crazy."

Adrienne grabbed the portrait of Theo and passed it to Tyler, then she grabbed Sir John's portrait and those of her parents. They were heavy and awkward, but between, Tyler and Adrienne , they managed to get them down and carry them out to the hallway.

"Quickly, my dear, there's no time to waste," Sir John commanded.

They made their way through the smoke and flames down the stairs to the front entrance and safety. They placed the pictures on the lawn and sat down to watch the flames engulf the old lady.

Adrienne sat in a daze. Her lovely home was burning to the ground. She and Tyler watched the firemen do their best to save the house. It was too old and burned rapidly like dry paper. Peter died with his obsession. Now she understood Hannah's words. There was no longer a Wyngate Manor.

* * * *

Three of the stone walls of the house stood as well as the columns supporting the roof over the main entrance. It wasn't until they were bulldozed that the 'Dead Man's Gold' was found in leather bags buried in the center of the columns. The bodies were identified only by their worn and tattered clothes. The fire hadn't invaded the lower caves.

Epilogue

Seven years later, at Hunter's Lodge, Tyler and Adrienne sat, enjoying a drink on the patio when their five-year-old daughter, Autumn came running to them.

"Mommy, Daddy, the man in the picture talked to me."

Adrienne and Tyler smiled at each other and laughed. "The old rogue is at it again."

The End

About the Author
June Bradley

June E. Bradley started writing in her late teens after seeing Daphne DeMuir's, 'Rebecca.' It reminded her of the many stately Mansions she saw every weekend in Newport Rhode Island.

Her family would often drive along Ocean Drive, and admire all the beautiful homes. She often wondered what secrets laid behind those tall stone walls and iron gates. Newport and the Navy still have a special place in her heart and influence her writing. Her husband retired after thirty years and she still misses that way of life.

After a long illness then the death of her husband she started writing again. June has two grown children, four grandchildren and resides in Chesapeake, VA.

She has one book published by Hardshell Word Factory through Mundania Press, called 'Shannon's Creek' which is a Paranormal Romantic.

Other Books by the author with Melange

An Elegant Swan